the
☒ BOYS'
club

Amanda Swift

SIMON &
SCHUSTER

SIMON &
SCHUSTER

First published in Great Britain by Simon & Schuster UK Ltd, 2004
A Viacom company

1 3 5 7 9 10 8 6 4 2

Simon & Schuster U
Africa House
64-78 Kingsway
London WC2B 6AH

A CIP catalogue record for this book is available from the British Library

ISBN 0 689 83754 2

Typeset by SX Composing DTP, Rayleigh, Essex
Printed and bound in Great Britain by Cox & Wyman Ltd, Reading

For Craig

Chapter One

The Boys' Club

There'd only be one rule – to stay friends and have nothing to do with girls. Oh, and of course it would be a secret.

'Your eyes are so deep I want to jump in and swim in them.'

Aren't those the most disgusting fourteen words you ever heard? OK, so they could be exciting in different sentences, like 'Let's go *deep*-sea diving' or 'Let's go ski-jumping.' But *those* words, in *that* order and coming out of my brother's mouth . . . ugh!

In any case, they don't make sense. You can't swim in someone's eyes, can you? You can swim at the Splash Centre, or in the sea, or, if you're really desperate, in the pond in my friend Sam's back garden, but you can't swim in Liz Benchley's eyes.

Don't get me wrong. Liz is OK. She's Sam's sister and when she was ten she used to let us spray her with our water pistols until her floral leggings were dripping. Unfortunately, she's fourteen now and she's got mixed up with my brother, Max. Literally.

At this precise moment they were in a heap on the sofa, a tangle of limbs and hair. You couldn't tell which jeans and T-shirt belonged to Max and which to Liz. It was impossible to see where one of them began and the other ended. They'd curled themselves into a ball and turned away from the world. That might be OK for a hedgehog, but not for my brother, who's captain of the table tennis team.

I suppose I could have gone somewhere else. But no, actually, I couldn't.

Max had the same idea: 'You could go somewhere else.'

Amazingly, he could still speak.

'No, actually, I couldn't.'

'It's only ads.'

'It's the Grand Prix.'

Max is spiky, and I don't just mean his nature. He has spiky hair and a pointy face. Where everything about me is round and floppy – hair, cheeks, clothes – everything about him is angular and direct and on the edge.

'But it's only ads.'

'But it's the Grand Prix.'

Max and I get stuck sometimes. We can go round for hours like this. Luckily he kept it short, because he wanted to dive back into Liz's eyes, but we did once row for three hours about a piece of toast.

Liz chipped in. '*We* could go somewhere else.'

'No, we couldn't. It's my room.'

'It's our telly.'

'It's a stupid house.'

All this was true, and we both knew it, so I'm not sure why we kept on telling each other. I had a tricky choice: either to watch the Grand Prix with the snogging cobras in my face or to go out.

In the pre-video age I would have agonised over that one for hours, but thanks to VHS I simply popped in a tape, at the same time relieving Max of a fiver that was slipping dangerously out of his pocket. I'd tell him later, when he'd unlocked his limbs.

I got the 71 bus to the castle. Obviously the castle wasn't always on a bus route. In the 1550s it was at the end of a muddy track, surrounded by fields, not by rows of houses and shops. Although I'm into history, I'm not into long muddy walks, so all in all I'm glad of route 71.

Not so glad of the company, though. It was like a giant version of Max's room. On top, which was the only place I could get a seat, I was surrounded by snogging couples. There was kissing, nibbling, stroking, whispering, giggling – and humming. (The humming turned out to come from a rather strange-looking man next to me.)

I don't want you to think I'm obsessed with snogging. I'm not always like this and I don't even enjoy being like this when I am. It's true that when I was younger I covered my eyes and groaned when they kissed at the end of *Robin Hood*, but that's normal for anyone under eight. I don't mind kissing in films now, because it's usually just once, at the end, and by then the stars have earned it. After two hours of running around and confusion and putting each other down, it's their reward for getting through it, like the CD I get after Grandma comes for Christmas.

But when it's places I go and people I know, then I mind. Home, the bus, the cinema, the park . . . Half my class, my cousins, Fred at fencing, Max . . . What's happened to everyone? A year ago I had friends. Everything was normal. It was so normal, I didn't even think of it as normal. What I mean is that I was living then, not watching myself live. I spent time with my friends, and we played football, or games on the computer, or . . . Well, to tell you the truth, I don't know what we did, because I don't remember, but that was what was so good about it. I didn't need to remember anything because I was . . .

I don't want to say this – it's admitting that things have changed and that makes me feel watery in my eyes – but I *have* to say it, because once the water's there, there's only one way it can go and that's out down your cheek.

. . . I was happy.

Everyone got off at the shopping centre. And there's another thing that's changed. Until recently every boy I ever knew hated shopping. A toy-shop maybe, a games shop possibly, a clothes shop for five minutes if your mum was threatening you and there were holes in all your jeans. And I don't mean fashion holes, I mean real holes in embarrassing places. But suddenly everyone's doing it. Not just going shopping, but going shopping HOLDING HANDS. I will say no more, except that this is something I am never ever going to do.

At least they'd all piled off the bus. Just me and the hummer were left on top. I wanted to move to a seat on my own but thought that would look rude. Instead I read my book so hard I couldn't read it at all. He started humming again. That did it. I had to show him I'd really had enough, so I moved a few centimetres away from him. I thought he'd taken the hint, because he got off at the next stop, but when I looked out of the window he was kissing a woman waiting there.

The castle is at the end of the line. It really shouldn't be there. I mean, *I* think it should be there, because I like it, but nobody expects it to be there, so they don't go. That's great for me, because it's usually empty and it's easier to imagine you're Robin Hood if you haven't got women with hard hair and shiny macs smelling the roses and buying flapjacks. If you turn off the high street and follow a track, you suddenly see the castle moat. I love the moat. It looks so deep and threatening, but it's actually really shallow and it's full of goldfish. I chucked them some chocolate chip muffin crumbs I found in my pocket as I went past.

Whenever I feel down I walk round the moat. Round and round until I've found the answer. I went round about twenty times once, when I didn't get a bow and arrow set for my birthday. It worked, because the palace curator felt sorry for me and bought me one from the gift shop. When Max broke my catapult kit, it didn't take many laps to find the answer: put all his CDs back in the wrong boxes. When Mum left Dad, I walked and walked, but the answer never came.

Today I was on my first lap when I found the answer. Not in my head, but standing in front of me. A knight in shining armour. It's not every day you see a knight in full medieval armour, not even at the castle, but to be honest I wasn't surprised. It's the Medieval Fayre soon and the Merry Men are doing one of their re-enactments. I'm not sure who this knight was. It could have been Terry, who works at the library, or Paul, who's a milkman. I know most of them because I went along to a talk on jousting once. Whoever it was, he was covered from head to toe in dazzling armour. He looked so alone, but so together as well. And he saved me. I know knights are meant to save damsels in distress and twelve-year-old boys don't qualify. This knight didn't sweep me up and carry me back to my castle. He didn't even come up to me, or talk to me, or 'do' anything at all. He just gave me an idea. I headed straight home and got the boys round.

'But I haven't got a full set of armour,' Sam said.

'Nor have I.' That was Ben.

'I could manage some shinpads.'

'I couldn't. My mum swapped them for a gravy boat. Quite a bargain, she said, even though the boat had a chip. But then the pads had a "lingering smell", according to her.'

Sam and Ben had got it all wrong, so I set them straight.

'I don't mean dress up in armour.'

'But you said, "Let's be like knights in armour."' Ben can be very literal.

'You can be very literal,' I told him.

'I know that, Joe. You've told me on average 3,000 times a year for the past ten years.'

'I didn't tell you 3,000 times when we were two. It wasn't in my vocabulary.' I can be very literal too.

'No,' Ben smirked. 'Your vocabulary was filled with variations on poo-poo head.'

'Have you got a screwdriver?'

That was Sam. He tends to enter the conversation at 90 degrees, due to the fact that he's always doing something with his hands. Mending, making or just happily pulling something apart and putting it back together again. Give or take a few bits.

'No,' I told him.

He looked a bit lost for a moment and then started dismantling his shoe.

'If you can remember back to the mists of two minutes ago, I said "like". "Like" knights in armour. Not, "Let's get down to the Fayre and find ourselves a breastplate."'

Sam and Ben are my best friends. That's why I'm crabby with them. We're all crabby with each other, but we don't really mean it. Well, I meant it once when I told Sam he was socially dysfunctional, but he was mending the hotplate at Pizza Please – so I was right. Right?

We've known each other for ever. Literally for ever. Our mothers were at birthing classes together. I'm afraid they bonded at a lecture on breast-feeding. Mum says they saw a lovely video of a Norwegian woman breast-feeding triplets. I'm sorry, but how is that lovely? Three babies, two breasts – there's always going to be a queue. Anyway, I don't feel very comfortable with the B-word. I feel even less comfortable when I think of me using my mum as a drinks dispenser.

Anyway, we'd all prefer to have met at a cinema club, or bowling, or even at Scouts, but the fact is we went on from birthing classes to the baby clinic, to toddler gym, to pre-school playgroup, and from there it was a hop to primary school, the park football team and, our latest social activity, eating Pop-Tarts.

Ben brought them in. He arranges all the practicalities in our lives, like food, drink and where to buy Doc Martens. I'm the ideas man. I have great ideas. I just have trouble getting them across. I tried again.

'Like I said, I saw this knight.'

'You said,' said Ben.

'And he looked so great, just on his own, cutting the air with his sword. I think we should be like that.'

'But you're not suggesting dressing up?' mumbled Ben, through the Pop-Tart.

'Do you want us to take up fencing?' Sam can be a bit literal too.

'No! I don't want us to *do* anything. I want us to *not* turn into Max.'

That really floored them. Sam stopped fiddling with his shoe and Ben let a lump of apple fall out of his gaping mouth.

What's happened to words? They used to be so easy. I could string them together without thinking, in sentences like 'Do you want to go to the park?' and in answers like 'Yeah.' Now, despite the fact that my report says I have a 'wide vocabulary', I never seem to have the words for what I want to say.

I was trying to tell the others that I wanted us never to be like Max and Liz. I didn't want us to lose what we had, what we'd always had and what I always wanted – our friendship. I'd lost all real contact with Max since he'd got entwined with Liz, and I didn't want to lose Sam and Ben. That knight made me think of men alone, without all the complications of women. There have always been men alone – in schools, in armies, in monasteries – and they've been OK, haven't they? I wanted us to set up a boys' club, and there'd be only one rule: to stay friends and have nothing to do with girls. Oh, and of course it would be a secret.

Eventually, after four Pop-Tarts and a few cans of a sports drink that apparently makes you as fit as a five-mile run, they got the idea.

'So you want to set up a boys' club that has nothing to with girls,' said Ben.

'But we already have nothing to do with girls,' said Sam.

'I know, but I want to make it formal,' I said.

'OK,' they both agreed.

That was it. We'd founded our club. It had been so simple. We decided to go out and celebrate this momentous event. We went back down to the castle, hoping to see the knight again, but just as we got there Paul was driving off in his milk float, his armour clanking against the gear stick. I wondered if he ever delivered the milk in full armour. It'd probably slow him down.

We leant over the wall and stared into the moat. I should have been feeling happy, because I'd started something exciting and positive and new, but I didn't. Instead I felt just like I had before I'd thought of the club – uneasy, not sure what was going to happen to us.

At that moment the little group of goldfish swam round the corner of the moat. One of them seemed to be slower than the others. Then I realised that he was dead and was just floating on the surface. Perhaps I'd killed him with my crumbs.

Chapter Two

Alex

I felt we were going to be friends. I was excited but a bit scared. That's probably because I haven't made a new friend for twelve years.

'I hereby open this meeting of the Boys' Club,' I announced. 'Sam, you do the minutes.'

'OK,' said Sam, looking at his watch. 'How long do you want to talk for?'

Before I could explain about taking minutes, there was a knock at the door. It was Mum. I don't know why she knocks, particularly as she then always comes straight in anyway, but that's just Mum.

'I wanted to let you know,' she started, but then the nightmare happened. Dad came in.

When I said Mum left Dad, I didn't mean that she left the house, or that we left the house, or even that he left the house.

Dad didn't knock. He's not a knocking person, except for knocking down walls. It's quite a frequent nightmare, this, although in theory they're not supposed to be around in the same place at the same time.

'I wanted to let you know, I'll be blasting a bit downstairs. Chest of drawers. Got to get it stripped by Monday.' Dad's a stripper. Furniture only.

When Mum and Dad designed the divorce house – yes, divorce house – they didn't think much about what would happen in the middle. They just thought it was a brilliant idea. They didn't *agree* it was a brilliant idea, because they never agree about anything, but it's undeniable that they both had the same idea, at the same time, and they both thought it was brilliant. We're good at ideas in our family and this was theirs: rather than buy separate flats, they'd keep the family house. Mum would live upstairs, Dad downstairs, with us kids in the middle. Max and I could spend time with Mum or with Dad, or be on our own, or be with each other, and Mum and Dad would never have to meet. The trouble with good ideas is that they often don't work in practice.

Part of the problem is the house. It's tall and thin, and there are only two rooms on the middle floor, one big and one small. Guess who has the big one? Big brother. OK, so they agreed that he would have a TV and a sofa in his room, and I'm allowed to watch the TV there. Guess how much trouble that causes? Yes, lots. But not nearly as much as the fact that Mum and Dad never worked out what to do if they should ever meet on the middle floor. They really need an elaborate intercom system. Sam could have done a great job. This would allow them to avoid each other, simply calling us up or down to their level.

Of course, they never thought to set up anything as sensible as that, and actually most of the time they don't run into each other. Mum pops down, Dad pops up and all is well. But occasionally we get these clashes and I wonder why they go on letting them happen. Maybe they secretly want to meet. Not so they can chat and find they get on now and fall in love all over again, like they would in some stupid film, but so they can see how many grey hairs the other has, or if they've put on weight, or if they've made unfortunate fashion choices.

This was a particularly unhappy encounter, because of the noise factor. Their needs were so different and they weren't going to budge.

'I'm leading a meditation on the placenta,' said Mum to me. Mum's a midwife. One of those ones who sorts out babies at home with the whole family watching. Well, just as long as I never have to.

'It's acrylic paint. It'll take some blasting,' said Dad to me.

I'm in the middle. Of the house and of their lives. They were both looking at me. Sam and Ben got on with other things. Staring, fiddling. They weren't embarrassed. They

14

were just waiting for something more interesting to happen.

Sometimes it's good being in the middle. Literally.

'We're going out,' I said to them both, 'so you won't disturb us.'

Mum and Dad hovered, as if they wanted it to be harder. They didn't really, but they didn't want it to be so easy. They'd got used to life being awkward. So in a way it was nice for them when something happened that made us all feel awkward. As Mum and Dad hovered in the doorway, Ben stared, Sam fiddled and I wondered if Robin Hood ever had this trouble with his parents. But then our attention was drawn towards Max's bed. The duvet started to move, not because of any mystery or magic, but because Max and Liz were lying underneath it, entwined. Sam, Ben and I were mildly surprised, because we'd been in there for a while, setting up our club meeting. We'd never bothered looking at Max's bed or wondering where he was. What really surprised me wasn't that we hadn't noticed them, but that they'd wanted to lie there kissing for that long. Something *else* I'll never do.

Mum and Dad looked a bit more than surprised. More like completely shocked and stunned. What did they think was going to happen? Max is fourteen and he doesn't have my mature attitude to the opposite sex. It was as if he'd changed overnight from a baby with carrot purée smeared on his face into a sex beast. In fact, there had been a few signposts along the way, like the Football Club disco, when he danced all night with the Under-Ten Girls' goalie, through to his fourteenth-birthday-party sleepover, to which he'd invited seven girls and me.

At least the Max and Liz situation distracted Mum and Dad. The tension between them faded and re-formed between them and their older son. They didn't do anything, of course, except mumble about urgent jobs they had to get on with, like watching the roses grow (Mum) and undercoating the cooker (Dad).

It didn't feel right to have the club meeting with the ultimate couple, Liz and Max, listening in, so we rescheduled it for the next day.

'What if the bus driver's a woman?' asked Ben, a bit confused. 'Do I ask for a ticket?'

I put him straight. 'Of course! You could get in trouble if you don't.'

Sam stopped walking to peer at a telephone cable box which had been left open. Unfortunately, this didn't take up all his brain space and he chipped in.

'You could mime. Pretend you're deaf.'

'That might not stop me falling in love.'

'True. We've got a deaf couple living next door.'

Luckily the bus came and brought with it a change of discussion. The driver was an old bloke of about forty, so there was nothing more to be said. Or so I thought, but the boys had got stuck in.

Sam first: 'But I've got a sister. Do I stop talking to her? She'll get the hump and stop giving me her cast-off computer games.'

Ben frowned. I've told him to stop doing this when he's worried or he'll end up looking like someone wrinkly from *Star Wars* by the time he's twenty, but it makes no difference. Ben's always worried. His forehead was full of furrows now, which is a bad sign. One line is mild concern about French homework, two is anxiety about the football results and three is mega matters of war, death, aliens and girls.

'What about girls at school? I'm on the chemistry bench with Marilyn.'

The dangers dawned on Sam. 'Natalie sometimes comes for a coffee with her mum. To our house!'

It was clear that our club needed a constitution. Ideally it should be written, but as we were on the bus on our way to Kingsland Comprehensive, which has at least 350 girls in it, of whom about fifty are potential targets for our misplaced adolescent affections, I had no time for drafts and documents. I had to tell them there and then.

'I don't mean avoid girls completely, like not talk to them, or not buy bus tickets off them. I mean don't fall in love.'

'Oh!' they both exclaimed, getting the point at last, but this immediately turned into 'Aaargh' as the bus lurched and the driver managed to bring it to rest just a short walk from our bus stop.

I don't know what it is with the bus driver. He stops there every day, but every day he nearly forgets. I think it's the sight of hundreds of black blazers and long lanky legs. Maybe he's scared of kids.

Mr Carson is. He peeps round the door to see what we're doing before he comes in. He's like a frightened little frog. Once he's checked the terrain isn't too terrifying, he hops over to his desk. He's so scared it actually stops us from scaring him, so in a way his terror is quite good for discipline. Someone should tell the school inspectors and they could make being nervous of children part of the government's education policy.

Once Mr Carson was in and we were sitting down – a process that should take about two minutes but with our class takes about ten while various people wander round looking for their desks – Mr C made an announcement.

Marilyn wouldn't be in and could Ben and I make a note of the homework and take round the right books after school? Ben glanced at me – was it safe?

Other people say Marilyn's very pretty. I've never looked, but I do remember that she used to be good at making up games in the garden, especially in the summer, when the tent and sandpit could be included. I'm afraid Marilyn's mum was in the birthing class too, so we've probably done embarrassing things together like play in the paddling pool with no clothes on. I don't want to think about it.

There was no chance to discuss this with Ben in private – we were about to start French – but, as I'd said on the bus, talking to girls was allowed, it was only falling in love that wasn't, and if Ben was with me, he wouldn't go in for a drink. If he *did* go in for a drink, then he probably would fall in love with her, but if we kept it to the doorstep it would be OK.

I didn't tell Ben any of this because Mr Carson was looking at us through his misty glasses, expecting us to say yes. Of course we did, not least because there was no way we were going to announce in front of the whole class that we'd given up girls. Well, not so much given up, just not given in.

At break there was time to discuss it, but we played football instead. It's much easier than talking about how you feel non-stop. I pretend that I've pushed all my feelings inside the ball and then I kick them away, as hard as I can.

Trouble is, I focus so intensely on kicking the ball, I don't pay much attention to where it's going. I looked up to see it landing on Big Bob's head. Not ideal. Unfortunately, Big Bob isn't like Robin Hood's friend Little John. We don't call him Big because he's little. We call him Big because he's big. Also, unlike Little John, he isn't on our side. He isn't on anyone's side. He's on his own side.

He picked up the ball and held it in his hands. He didn't move, so I bravely took a step towards him. He didn't move. I took another step. Unfortunately, this was through a puddle. A Kingsland special. Full of spittle and chewing-gum. I splashed my way through it. Then he did something weird. He turned and ran into school, throwing the ball back over his shoulder as he went.

Takes all sorts, I guess.

When I got back to the classroom I felt about as excited as I always *don't* before double RE. School is just so predictable. Lesson, lesson, break, lesson, lesson, lesson, lunch break, lesson, lesson, lesson, fight, home. For once, something surprising happened. Or rather, someone.

There was a new boy sitting in our class. New boys in

themselves aren't so exciting. We get them now and then at the beginning of the year. But this wasn't the beginning of the year, or even the term, or even the day. And this boy did look exciting. I don't know why.

He was sitting in the front desk, the one we all avoid. He was small, but he looked strong. He had short black hair and he was writing. When I came in he looked up and for some reason I noticed he had very black eyes. Not bruised, just black and deep. He looked at me for a moment, then went back to his writing.

'This is Alex Bobinski,' announced Mr Carson with the usual tremble in his voice. 'He'll be with us for a few weeks, while the circus is in town.'

Some people laughed. I wondered if Mr Carson had flipped. Had ten years of teaching at Kingsland turned on the nutty switch in his head? Alex suddenly got up and walked towards the door. Was he going to be a door-slammer? We've had a few of those, as well as shouters, chalk-throwers and weedy-wet-weepers. When Alex got to the door he suddenly turned round, put his hands up in the air and flung himself forward into this amazing sequence of backflips and somersaults, right across the front of the class. He ended with a little bounce, then walked back to his desk. Everyone was quiet, for the first time in a year or two.

Alex was sitting on his own at lunch, so I went over to him.

'Do you perform in the circus?'

'Not very much. In a year or two I'll be a Bouncing Bobinski, but I need to bounce a bit better first.'

'You bounced OK across the classroom.'

'I don't like to show off, but I have to let people see what I can do before they can tell me where to go.'

His English was really good but he spoke with an accent. 'Where are you from?'

'Bydgoszcz.'

'Oh, yeah,' I said, as if I knew where it was.

'It's in Poland. We export garlic sausage and acrobats.'

He smiled at me, a big smile that rippled up to his eyes. I felt strange and wondered why, but then I realised it was because Natalie was standing next to me. That must have been it. I used to be able to stand quite close to girls and feel OK. Now I get sick and sweaty. I think maybe I'm allergic to their deodorant.

'Joe, it's the school debate next week, on Wednesday. Will you speak, with Sam as your second?'

Natalie's incredibly direct. She always has been. She once told me I smelt of eggs (I had hard-boiled ones in my packed lunch) and wrote to my mother, asking her to give me different sandwiches. She even enclosed a list of suggested fillings. That's direct, isn't it? Especially for an eight-year-old. She's twelve now and nothing's changed.

'The subject is "Schools Should be Single Sex." You're speaking for. It's at 4.30 in the common room.'

I tried to answer. 'The thing is, Natalie—' But she'd gone. I looked back at Alex. 'She doesn't take no for an answer. In fact, she doesn't take an answer for an answer.'

He laughed. I felt we were going to be friends. I was excited but a bit scared. That's probably because I haven't made a new friend for twelve years.

Chapter Three

The Midnight Thrash

We carried on like that until three, and by then of course we'd finished all our varieties of cereal except the yukky nutty one . . .

'What's the point in making friends with Alex? He'll be gone in a few weeks.' Ben was being literal again.

I put him straight. 'That's like saying, "What's the point in chatting to someone on the bus? You may never see them again."'

'Exactly. The other day this woman on the bus asked me about my school uniform. I'd far rather have stared out of the window and thought about the Cup Final.'

'Anyway, I might not end up friends with him. Three weeks isn't very long.'

'Exactly. That's what I meant.'

That was the end of that discussion. It would probably have ended on its own, but it had to stop because we'd got to Marilyn's door. Marilyn answered it. She's always been a bit different, Marilyn. Or looked different anyway. She wears more than she really needs to, in layers. Like a skirt over trousers, over tights, and a T-shirt, vest, cardigan and jacket. There are always lots of different materials involved too, like denim and leather and velvet and stuff with patterns on. She has her hair in loads of little plaits and there are other things dotted about in it, like miniature flowers and butterflies. Not live ones, of course – it'd be a lot of feeding and watering if they were, and I guess her hair would drip. I don't usually notice what people look like, but we had to write a description of a person once in English. I wrote about Marilyn because we had to do a whole page and there's a lot to say about her. If I had to write about Ben and Sam it'd be over in half a line because I'd just put, 'He looks OK.'

Today she was wearing the usual layers and nature table on her head, but there was something different about her. She was carrying a bundle of blankets. When it started squawking, I realised it was a baby.

'Why didn't you come to school?' asked Ben.

'My mum's just had Pom-Pom,' she said, indicating the bundle. 'I'm helping out for a bit.'

There was a loud, deep bellow from upstairs, like a distressed whale. I looked at the baby. It seemed as if Marilyn's mum had already given birth to it, so why was she wailing now?

Marilyn blushed. 'She's got to keep up her singing. She's got a gig at the weekend.'

'Is that singing?' asked Ben.

'It's experimental,' said Marilyn. Did that mean it was or it wasn't?

The baby started to cry. It was clearly time to go. Ben handed the work over, laying it gently on the baby's stomach.

'Here's your homework. Maths is for Friday, English is for Monday, physics is for when we feel like it.'

Marilyn smiled. 'Is that true?'

'No, but it'd be nice, wouldn't it? It's for Wednesday.'

'Thanks,' she said. 'Would you like a drink?'

Oh, it had all been going so well! Just a few words, the job done and we'd be off. Now we were confronted with the nightmare situation of being invited in! We both knew the dangers, and we both knew what we had to say – something simple, like 'No thanks.' For some reason that didn't happen, but something else did. We ran away. Like a couple of kids playing Knock and Run. OK, we'd achieved our aim of not having a drink and therefore not entering into a major relationship with Marilyn. On the other hand, we'd been really childish and stupid. Worst of all, would she wonder what was up with us and somehow find out about the club? We wanted to know, and yet we didn't want to find out.

When I got home I felt really embarrassed. There's nothing odd about that, since I feel embarrassed during most of my waking hours. Most of the time I have no idea what exactly I'm embarrassed *about*, but this time I knew exactly what it was: I was embarrassed because we'd run away.

And there was another feeling. (Two at once – how deep!) I was worried. I was worried that the club was not getting off to a good start. It seemed to be making us have more to do with girls, not less. And what we did have to do with girls was, well, embarrassing. I had to do something before my cheeks got so red and hot, they set fire to my nose. What we needed was a controlled environment. A place where girls wouldn't, maybe even *couldn't*, get in: the changing rooms at school, the showers at the swimming pool, the gents' toilet at the football ground . . . I immediately sensed a problem. These might be girl-free, but they weren't exactly places where you'd want to spend more than the thirty seconds it takes to change, pretend to wash or pee. We'd have to control our space by more subtle methods, like a sign on my bedroom door saying NO GIRLS!!!

No. That would be sexist and I might be taken to a

court of human rights. How could I arrange it so that Sam, Ben and I could have a boys' club meeting without it turning into an all-night mixed rave (complete with snogging in dark corners and the airing cupboard)?

There was my clue. I had just thought of it without *thinking* of it. ALL NIGHT. Not a rave and not mixed sex, of course, but if we met at *night*, in the middle of the night, there was very little chance we'd be interrupted.

That's what we'd do then. But what would we actually do? Sleep? Eat? Measure our spots? The answer didn't come to me for two whole days. And even when it did, it didn't seem like the answer. It seemed more like Max and his music waking me up at six minutes past two in the morning. Max's favourite radio programme is *Mikey and Mike's Midnight Thrash*. That's OK. In fact, it's my favourite programme too. But it's only my favourite programme when I'm listening to it, not when I'm flat out, having a very pleasant dream about beating Max at chess.

I was about to bang on the wall and do my tortured little brother act when I had my big idea: the Boys' Club Midnight Thrash. Perfect. I e-mailed Sam and Ben. I e-mailed Mum and Dad so that they couldn't complain that they hadn't had the same information or been told first. I e-mailed Tesco and ordered three variety packs of cereal and twelve pints of milk.

I arranged everything for Saturday. No point staying up all night and sleeping all day at school. You might as well stay awake at home all day and show off about how tired you are.

The boys came round at ten. We turned off our mobiles so we wouldn't be enticed out to any mixed parties. We spent a while drumming on our knees. Then we chose our Fantasy Football Team, selecting only from players who've been sent off this season. Then we did a bit of star-gazing, because I've got an old poster of the night sky on my wall. We drew in a really good constellation of a police heli-copter. Then the magic hour struck. Midnight. As Mikey and Mike started to yell, we were on the bed, on my chair, on my bean-bag, jumping and thrashing and punching the ceiling. Mum wasn't around to complain – she was at a vigil for victims of bad dentistry. She'd left Dad to complain, and he never does. During the ads we flopped down and tore open a variety pack. We sploshed on the milk and then it was a desperate race to see who could finish before the next track. It was brilliant.

We carried on like that until three, and by then of course we'd finished all our varieties of cereal except the yucky nutty one, so we tore those open and tried to stuff it down each other's shirts. Then Mum came in. She'd come back early because they'd moved on to the victims of dentures and she can't relate to them. Also, I think she wanted to make sure we went to bed. We were feeling rebellious, so we didn't do what she said. OK, so we went to bed, but we didn't brush our teeth or change out of our clothes.

The thrash was a huge success. I knew it was, because both Ben and Sam said 'Later' when they left. Usually they don't say anything at all.

Flushed (but not embarrassed) with the success of the thrash, I decided the Boys' Club really could work, but we had to keep out of the way of girls. Most of the time that's not too difficult. We stand around in different parts of the playground, we sit at separate tables at lunch, we don't work in the same groups unless a teacher who's taller than us tells us we must. I could go for weeks without talking to a girl at all.

Then I remembered the debate.

I realised I had to get us boys out of it. I really couldn't risk a big mixed event like that. I decided to go straight up to Natalie on Monday morning and tell her we weren't doing it.

I did go up to her, but before I had a chance to say anything she started firing commands at me. Commands like: 'Ten minutes opening speech, five minutes second.' And: 'Put up this poster.' I had no ammunition.

Anyway, I have to admit I was interested in the subject, but it was tricky. I didn't want anyone to think I don't like girls, because I don't. I mean I do. I do like them. I don't not like them. It's just that I feel sick when I'm near them, and I've got enough queasy situations coming up in the next few years: GCSEs, watching Arsenal and England in various cups, leagues and championships, as well as the times when I really am sick. I can't cope with any more. I wrote a few notes, about different interests, leisure activities, boys' need for space, girls' need to talk. Does that sound sexist? It's true. When we play football, they all stand round the edge of the playground talking. Sometimes they *walk* round the edge of the playground talking. Sam says that when Liz has been out for the day with her girlfriends, she rings them up when she gets home and they talk about how it went.

Sam and I had a quick chat about what we were going to say, but we didn't make much effort. We didn't care about winning because we didn't want to do it in the first place.

On the day of the debate we went down to the girls' common room after school. Marilyn was back, with some new little koalas climbing up her plaits. Ben had come along and so had Alex. There weren't many other boys there, which wasn't surprising, because the debate clashed with

Computer Games Club, but there was one boy there who was a total surprise: Big Bob. He'd never been to a debate before. He doesn't really believe in verbal exchanges, just physical ones. He was lounging at the back, staring across the room. I looked to see what he was staring at. It was Natalie.

She didn't notice him because she was looking over her speech. The room filled up. The front row was a long line of long bare legs, all belonging to Kingsland girls. Don't they get cold? You couldn't help noticing all the legs because they were stretched out and crossed over and twisted under each other. Girls' skirts hitch up and you think you're going to see their pants, and you really don't want to look, but something compels you to stare.

Once I saw the audience, I wished I'd prepared. I'd only written about ten lines on my card. What came in between? My mouth felt dry but I was sweaty all over. I hadn't realised Liz would be speaking for the motion as well as Natalie. She did really well. Of course she did, because she wants to spend all day snogging Max and they've got more chance if they're in the same building.

I stumbled through my bit, but I made them laugh a couple of times with my descriptions of boys doing belly-dancing and going cross-eyed doing cross-stitch. Natalie, of course, was very direct and very convincing. I don't know why she bothers with school. She ought to be given special permission to be the country's youngest-ever head teacher. She'd be better than our head, who spends all his time on courses and occasionally pops into school for a coffee.

Then it was Sam's turn. Sam's usually good at talking, especially if he's got something to fix at the same time. When it's just him, Ben and I, we sometimes can't shut him up until the plug's back in its socket. He got up to speak. Natalie whispered something to her friend and the friend laughed. Sam noticed and started to shuffle on his feet, as if he'd suddenly discovered he had an extra leg he didn't need. He got out his notes from his pocket. They were crumpled into a little ball, which he carefully flattened with his stubby fingers. Everyone went very quiet. What would he say?

He shuffled a bit more, studied his notes and looked at Natalie, who gave him a stern look back. 'Before I start,' said Sam, 'there's something I have to finish.' He got a watch and a tiny screwdriver out of his pocket and he started to mend the watch.

At first people thought it was a gimmick and they made a few comments. Then they thought it was a joke and they started to laugh. In the end they wanted him to get on with it and they started to clap, slowly and in time. Sam didn't seem to notice anything. He peered at the watch, trying to work out what was wrong. Natalie looked increasingly cross. In the end she declared the debate over. We lost.

I gave Sam hell on the way home. 'What did you do that for?'

He looked as if he might cry. I didn't want him to do that, but I didn't want him to do what he did in the debate either.

'Natalie was looking at me. Everyone was looking at me. I suddenly felt that I had to fix the watch.'

'Did you manage it?' I asked, a bit more kindly.

'No. It's had it.'

He took the watch out of his pocket again and slung it in a skip we were walking past. That's unlike him. He usually keeps every bit of everything in case he can use it for something else. He didn't come back to my house. Often we hang out after school together, but that day neither of us felt like it.

I had tea with Mum. Max was there too, and he really enjoyed telling her about the debate in great detail, dwelling on Sam's weird performance. She obviously found it funny but didn't want me to know, because she wouldn't look at me while she was doing the washing-up but I could see her shoulders shaking.

After tea I went out for a walk. It was dusk and I'm not really supposed to be out on my own when the street-lights are on, but it's my birthday in a few months and I think the rule should change. There are things I'd do at nearly thirteen that I'd never have considered at twelve, like wearing aftershave. To be honest, I'm still considering it and not doing it, because I'd like to be sure I won't go round whiffing like a gone-off skunk.

I wandered up to the heath. It always makes me feel better to be up there. The sparkling views of the town, the sharp evening air, even the headlights of the cars sliding out of town calm me down. The circus was on the other side of the heath and I wandered over. I've always wondered whether circus people live in their caravans all year or if they have houses too. I realised I could ask Alex now.

The show was on, so the site was empty. I could hear the drum rolls and crashes of cymbals, and the audience applauding at I didn't know what. A horse on two legs, a bendy lady, maybe Alex's mum and dad and the rest of them. Most of the caravans were empty and I walked cautiously between them, wary of the big dogs that lurked there, ready to leap out on their leads and scare any intruders. At the far side of the site was a huge caravan, empty and lit up. I could see a living-room at one end with a big TV and lots of knick-knacks and family photos, like any other family home. I walked right round the caravan, looking in at the window. On the other side there was a tumbling Alex. It was an amazing sequence, even in the half-light. He reached the end, turned round and saw me. He was hostile at first.

'Did you see the show?'

'No. I'd like to.'

'Don't,' he said. 'My parents are not getting on and it's making the act bad.'

'Oh,' I said unhelpfully. 'Are they going to split up?' I tried to imagine a divorce caravan.

'No,' he said. 'In the summer they always row. Mum wants to go back home and Dad wants to stay on the road.'

'What do you want to do?'

'I don't mind. I don't have time to make friends, even at home, because we're only there for a few weeks' holiday and then we go off again.'

'But they're there when you get back.'

'Yeah. But they're older by then and I've missed so much.'

'It's like if you only watch a soap once in a while,' I said. 'You can work out what's going on but you can't really enjoy it.'

'Yeah,' he said vaguely, glancing a bit nervously at the tent.

I wanted him to invite me into the caravan but I didn't want to *ask* him to. I was uncomfortable but I didn't want to go home.

'I'm sorry about today. The debate.'

'It was good. I liked what you said.'

'Yeah, but what about Sam?'

'There is not much I can say about mending a watch.'

He laughed and I had to laugh too. It made me feel better. Alex stopped laughing and looked straight at me.

'Why did he do that?'

It was as if he knew about the club. Obviously he didn't, but now I wanted him to. I should have asked the others first, but I had to tell him now.

'We have a kind of agreement . . .' I petered out. Was this a good idea?

'Yes?' said Alex encouragingly.

'We've decided – Sam, Ben and I – not to have anything to do with girls.' I held my breath. Was he going to laugh at me?

'That is a brilliant idea!' he exclaimed.

I smiled. I was so relieved. We could still be friends and I could still keep the club going. If he'd thought the idea was stupid, he might have told the whole school. He started dancing about, doing little gymnastic steps and jumps.

'I have been thinking about that too! When I was younger, it never was a problem if you were a boy or girl. We all wore jeans and didn't brush our hair. I was friendly with boys and girls. But now it has all changed. People who were friends don't know how to talk to each other any more.'

'Exactly!' I joined in, but not with the hopping about.

'The girls spend all their time dressing up and making up. I hate it, that girls are like that, and boys are drowning in hair gel.'

Wow. This was a first: he had even stronger opinions than me.

'It's just the same here,' I said.

'I have decided a little time ago that I do not wish to be like that,' he said, looking serious.

'So have I!'

It was amazing. It was as if he'd been reading my mind as he trundled across Europe in his caravan. I dropped my guard.

'We've formed a club . . .'

He jumped on the idea, and in the air.

'Can I join?'

My mouth opened and the words came out, 'Yeah, of course.'

There was a huge round of applause from the big top.

The sound seemed to change him and he became stiff and tense.

'You'd better go,' he said.

I didn't want to. I felt we'd just become real friends and ought at least to have a can of Fanta to celebrate.

'Don't you want to talk about the club?'

'Not now. At school tomorrow.'

He turned me round and practically marched me down the hill. When I came to the road, I looked back. He was leading a white pony away from the tent. He took a huge leap, landed in the saddle, lifted the reins and galloped off across the heath.

Chapter Four
Ben and Marilyn

'I've said I'll go round to Marilyn's . . . She wants some butterflies on Pom-Pom's cot.'

'I've asked Alex to join the club.'

Ben didn't answer. Was he angry? I didn't know. He flicked over and butterflied off down the pool. I caught up with him at the other end.

'Is that OK with you?'

He didn't answer. He was too out of breath. Or was he? Perhaps he was pretending to be out of breath because he was angry.

'Stop yakking like a couple of girlies and hit your target!' Mr Price bellowed from the other end of the pool.

That did it. Accused of being girlies! We shot off like potato pellets from a spud gun.

'And BREATHE!!' he screamed. 'Or else I'll hold your breath for you! That'll teach you to breathe when you've got the chance!'

Mr Price is quite an unusual teacher. A bit of a dinosaur. Apparently lots of teachers used to be like this, but these days they're not allowed to. They have to write little smiles on the blackboard and send you a Christmas card instead. Mr Price doesn't do anything like that. He shouts. He screams. He bellows. He goes bright red in the face and loses his voice. He tells us to be competitive and aggressive. He bribes and blackmails us. It's really awful. Not because we don't like it, but because it works. When I went to Swimming Club I could do half a width if I put my foot on the bottom three times. It wasn't really swimming, it was more like long-distance hopping. After three weeks at the club I could do hundreds of lengths. Literally.

I can't tell my mum. I mean, I can tell her about the lengths, but not about the lengths Mr Price goes to to get us to swim them. She'd take me out of the club. Mum thinks everything in life should be soft and gentle and nice. She likes deep-breathing, but not the sort we do at swimming. When we do our deep-breathing, it gets us to the other end of the pool faster than a torpedo. Mum does her deep-breathing sitting still on the bed. What on earth is the point of that? She says it helps her deal with her anger with Dad. Yes, it does, as long as she's sitting on the bed. As soon as she stops deep-breathing and stands up, she's furious all over again.

I tried talking to Ben at the other end.

'So is it OK with you? I mean, we had such fun the other night, and with an extra person . . .'

'Yeah, if that's what you want,' he managed, before he torpedoed off again.

What did that mean? That it wasn't what *he* wanted? If only we were like dolphins and could communicate subtle sonic messages under water. All I can do is recognise Ben by his goggles and perhaps show him how many lengths I've swum by holding up my fingers. A dolphin could probably tell you where the dangerous fishing nets are, how many miles it is to Ireland and where to pick up the best tuna.

I decided to talk to Ben after swimming, but the changing rooms were too public. I'd have had to shout over the cubicle and unravel my pants at the same time. I hate the way your clothes get all twisted up at swimming. Sometimes it almost puts me off going, but I love being in the water. Mum says it's because I was three weeks early and I'm trying to recapture those lost days in the amniotic sac, but I think it's because swimming doesn't make you sweaty. That's what I hate about running. It makes you all sweaty and out of breath. Max loves being sweaty and out of breath. That's why he likes table tennis, and snogging Liz, I guess.

Also I couldn't talk about the club in the changing

rooms, because the other club (I mean the Swimming Club) members would have heard, and that would have got us into some serious trouble.

As soon as we got into the pool's ticket hall I took a deep breath, ready to start talking again, but up came Mr Price.

'Sorry to interrupt,' he whispered. He was all bent over and humble. 'Are you two boys all right?'

Mr Price isn't a full-time shouter. He always regrets it afterwards. Then you have to go through this silly ritual of making him feel OK about it.

'Yeah, we're fine,' we chorused.

'Beat my best time tonight,' said Ben encouragingly.

'Yes, yes,' said Mr Price, as if he wasn't sure this was a good idea. 'Well, I must be off to my kick-boxing. See you next week.'

He sloped off in the direction of the gym, looking uncomfortable with himself. He was always like this after the class on Thursdays, but by next week he'd be back to bellowing again.

Walking back home, we were able to talk. We often do our talking when we're walking. Perhaps it's because we're doing something else as well, or not looking at each other. When I see people walking along, talking to themselves, I sometimes wonder if they were talking to a friend a few miles back and got so involved in what they were saying they didn't notice the friend had gone off to get some chips.

'Don't you like Alex?' I ventured.

'Yeah, he's OK,' muttered Ben.

Not exactly wild enthusiasm, I thought, but it would do for now.

'So shall I invite him along to the meeting on Saturday?'

'Yeah, but—' He stopped to look at a football bobbing down the river, but I knew he wasn't really looking at it. 'I'm not sure I can make it.'

I was stunned. 'Why not? It's not the Swimming Gala or the Arts Festival or your mum's compulsory biannual school-shoe-buying trip?' I paused. His brow was settling into the usual anxious furrows. I made one last guess. 'Have you been selected to play for Arsenal?' He laughed, but the furrows were still deeply set.

'I've said I'll go round to Marilyn's.'

I was shocked into momentary silence. 'What on earth for?' I said eventually, quite sharply.

'She wants some butterflies on Pom-Pom's cot.'

'So? She can run round the garden catching them, then glue them on.'

'She wants me to paint them.'

'But it's not even her baby.' I was pointing out the obvious.

'It's her half-sister.' So was he.

'Exactly. If the baby needs butterflies, then her mum can sort them out.'

'That's the point. Marilyn's mum is really busy with her recording. She's got to get eight tracks down by the end of the month.'

'That shouldn't take long. If I wailed like that, I could get it done in a couple of hours.'

He didn't answer. I began to feel really scared. Was he not only turning into a soppy cot-decorator but also learning to love Marilyn's mum's singing?

'There must be someone else who can do it.'

'There isn't.'

We walked along in silence for a bit. Now we weren't so much like mad people talking to themselves as sad people not talking to each other. I couldn't work it out. It was as if Ben and Marilyn had skipped all the discos, parties and hours and hours spent standing and flirting on the street, and had jumped straight on to the square marked parenthood. Working backwards, this must mean our joint resolve had already been broken. He had fallen for her.

'Have you—'

'No!' he jumped in before I could finish. 'I haven't fallen for her. I'm doing it for the baby.'

Now that one I hadn't seen coming. I'm usually very good at guessing the endings. Who's going to die, who's going to kiss, who's going to end up with their face in a cream cake and their feet in a chandelier.

'But you're nothing to do with the baby. It's not like you're its dad.'

'I am,' he announced assertively, and then, a bit less certainly, 'sort of.'

This was as crazy as the time he jumped off his shed roof into the rose bush. He was wearing a Superman outfit at the time, but even so. Just as I remembered his mum dabbing his thorn-pricked back with witch hazel, I remembered something else: that Ben had never had a dad. Not one that he could remember. Could it be that he wanted to be like a father to this baby? I was amazed, mainly at how clever I'd been to work it out. I decided to change my tune, and my tone. Mum says I can be bossy, like Dad is, and though she's saying it partly to get at Dad, she's actually right.

'So you sort of want to be around?' I said in my quiet, not-so-bossy voice.

'Yeah, and I sort of want to do the butterflies,' he said, looking unhappy but not quite so worried, which I know is quite a complicated way to look, but then Ben's quite a complicated person.

We had got to our road and it felt right to go our separate ways, at least for the next few minutes. Maybe he wanted to work out his butterfly design, or ask his mum why his dad left. I decided not to enquire.

'See ya,' I said in an uncomplicated way.

'Yeah,' he said, leaping up the stairs to his house and looking much happier. 'I think painted ladies would be nice—'

'I thought you were painting the cot, not Marilyn and her mum,' I quipped.

I thought he might laugh at my little joke, but he'd already gone through his watermelon-coloured front door.

Chapter Five
The Party Plan

We decided to have the party the next day, because it was Saturday and that's when you have parties, even ones without girls.

'Home-made lemonade and chocolate chip cookies?'

Sam's mum is unreal. At other people's houses you get a can of something fizzy and a packet of crisps, but Sam's mum lives to bake. She once got up at five in the morning to go and buy some sugar strands for his birthday cake. She drives out to the country to get her eggs straight from the farm. She buys flour from the mill. She once iced a chocolate sponge with a very lifelike representation of a mountain troll.

'Both, please,' I said, about the lemonade and the cookies.

'Sam?'

Sam didn't answer, which I know is rude, but not actually when you consider that he most likely didn't hear what his mum was saying. When he's really involved in making something, he doesn't talk or eat for hours.

Christmas is a particular problem, because he's always given something to make, so he misses Christmas lunch – and tea too, if the something is tricky. I usually go round to his house and eat his meals for him. It's only fair to his mum, who's spent days cooking.

She brought lemonade and cookies for two but he didn't eat, drink or look up. He's making a robot that can follow you to school, carrying your school bag, lunch-box, PE kit and cagoule. It can be programmed to bring you the right things at the right time of day, even down to the right-subject homework, or an original excuse if you haven't done it. Obviously this is a big project, the biggest Sam's ever attempted, and it's in the early stages. At the moment it's mainly flywheels and a glazed look in his eyes.

'I've asked Alex to join the club.'

No answer. Had he heard? Could he hear? Did he care? I tried again, and again, and again. I didn't know which was worse, feeling that he resented Alex or that he'd rejected me. Was he doing this to annoy me or had he gone bonkers about his 'bot? Suddenly the not knowing really, really got to me and I did something I really, really should not have done. While he was staring boggle-eyed at all the bits in front of him, I placed my fingers gently over one of the flywheels at the edge of his fixed field of vision, slid it towards me and then popped it into my pocket.

I left soon after. I couldn't believe what I'd done. Stealing – and from a friend! I felt terrible. I made myself feel better by deciding it wasn't really stealing. It was long-term borrowing in order to teach him a lesson. I decided I'd feel even better if I confessed to someone.

Alex laughed, but he stopped abruptly when I told him I thought that Sam and Ben didn't want him to join the club.

'Then maybe I should not join.'

'That's not fair,' I said. 'It doesn't give me the chance to go on and on at them until they change their minds.'

'Yes, but you and Sam and Ben are old friends. I do not want to get in the way.'

Actually he was, but only in the way of me and the TV. We were watching the gymnastics. Well, I was watching. He was leaping about trying to copy a twelve-year-old bendy Pole.

'You must join. We need more members. It's not much of a club with three. More of a triangle.'

'OK, then. I'll come along tomorrow. Is it morning or afternoon?'

'Neither,' I replied sadly. 'Ben can't come.'

'So are you going to change the day?'

'I might not bother. I don't think the others are very interested.'

'Maybe your script reading doesn't interest them.'

'How can they not be interested in Robin Hood's teenage years?'

'Perhaps they've heard it before?' he said kindly.

He was right. I'd only known Alex two weeks and I'd already read him my film script twice. He must have guessed that the others had heard it dozens of times.

'Perhaps you should do something a bit more fun. With food and drink,' Alex suggested.

'A medieval banquet? I can't roast a hog, but I guess I could do ham sandwiches.'

'Why don't you have a party?'

'Yes, but most people's parties these days have – you-know-what – girls.'

'Exactly,' said Alex. 'You can show it's possible to have a great party without you-know-whats.'

He did a funny little wiggle, leaned forward and smiled right in my face. His hair smelt really unusual, but nice. Like Sam's mum's lemonade.

'We could play chess . . .' I ventured.

'Yes, and have music, and food and drink, like any good party.'

He seemed really keen on the idea, and I must say I felt much happier too. We decided to have the party the next day, because it was Saturday and that's when you have parties, even ones without girls. Also, by then Ben would have done enough butterflies for the day. Sam wouldn't have finished the robot, but we'd all have left home for college by the time he did, so it wasn't practical to wait. After the gymnastics, we made a list of things to do. Alex got all enthusiastic about making blinis and other Polish treats that sound as if they're named after gymnasts. I went quiet again. Alex noticed.

'What's the problem now?' he asked, with just a tiny hint of irritation in his voice. I didn't blame him. It's not easy being with me. But it's not easy *being* me either.

'You know what we have to do first of all?' I said gloomily.

'Decide what to wear?'

I hoped he was joking. But I wasn't joking when I said, 'We have to ask Max if we can have the room.'

I gave him a look like people do in films when they have to climb Everest in sandals. Before I had a chance to tell Alex about the time I asked Max if I could watch a film when I was ill, and he shouted so loudly at me that Mum erupted and said he wasn't allowed to go and stay with Granny in Wales (I think that's partly why he did it), Max came in. With Liz, of course. They looked as if they were doing a three-legged race and all their limbs were tied together, including their heads. There wasn't a chink of light between their bodies. They slid over to the bed and fell on it, as if love had relieved them of the ability to stand up. I decided to ask straightaway, before he got grumpy with us for being in the room.

'Joe,' he growled. He was revving up.

'Max,' I said quickly, 'can I have the room tomorrow night?'

Silence. Anything could have happened in that moment. I wouldn't have been surprised if a small nuclear missile had winged its way over to me from the bed. I held my breath.

'Yeah,' he said, 'sure. We're going away.'

It wasn't a missile. It was honeysweet news from my snogging big brother. Alex and I were happy to leave him to it and set off for the Polish deli.

I hadn't given a party for ages. Not since the jelly and ice-cream kind. I didn't want a whole lot of boys from school coming over. For my birthday I prefer to go on an outing with just a few friends. Often it's Ben and Sam. In fact, it's always them. Other boys might not be interested in the kind of outings I choose. Last year it was a trip to Nottingham, where we went round the castle and then followed the Merry Men's Trail round Sherwood Forest. It was raining and we got lost, but I really enjoyed it.

This party was different. It was more of a grown-up

party, though of course without any girls. It was also different because Alex was helping me get ready for it. He was even more enthusiastic than I was. I mean, he showed it more than I did, by talking fast and writing lists and hopping about on the way back from the shops. I think he would have done a backflip if he hadn't had a rucksack on his back. I don't really show my enthusiasm in that kind of way. For a start, I can't do backflips. I prefer to do subtle things, like smile out of the corner of my mouth and maybe put on a clean T-shirt.

On Saturday morning Alex brought over his mum's recipes and spread them out all over our kitchen, along with the ingredients. I had suggested doing the cooking at his caravan, because he had all the herbs and spices there. Of course, that wasn't the real reason. I wanted to see what his room and his family were like. He said no, the caravan was too small and his parents were going through a bad patch due to a new jump his dad wanted his mum to do. She didn't think she was up to it.

So we did the cooking at my place. Mum didn't mind. I think she was quite pleased to meet a new friend of mine. She likes Ben and Sam, but she has seen them nearly every day for the last twelve years and on quite a few of those days, particularly in the first few years, they were crying, or being sick, or having tantrums. More recently, they've been quieter. Mum thinks they're too quiet, but that's because she's always asking embarrassing questions like 'Are you using deodorant yet?' No wonder they're quiet, with questions like that.

Alex seemed happy to chat to Mum, though. About the cooking, and being Polish, and life in the circus. Mum got all keen on the circus and suggested going along to watch, but Alex said no, it wasn't a good idea at the moment, due to his parents' problems with the act. Mum was a bit surprised, but she understands about parents with problems. She is one.

As soon as the cooking was done, Alex had to shoot off. He has to sell programmes and hot dogs at the show. I did the washing-up, which was a bit tricky, because I make a big stink about doing it after Mum's cooked, but I didn't mind doing it for Alex. Mum hovered about, fiddling with bits of pastry as if it were Playdoh. I thought she was going to tell me off about doing the washing-up, or rather not doing it when she asked, but she didn't. She seemed in a good mood. Maybe all those herbal remedies she's forever trying are finally starting to work. I don't like them because they stink, but who cares about the house smelling of cabbage if Mum's in a good mood?

'He seems nice,' she said, as she made a shape out of pastry. I think it was a heart.

'Yeah,' I said. I knew I wasn't saying much, but there wasn't much else to say. He is nice. Full stop.

'He's handsome, isn't he?'

'Is he?' I pretended I hadn't noticed. In fact I had.

'Yes. He's got a very gentle face.'

'Has he?' I said, scrubbing at a baking tin.

'Yes, he has,' said Mum, and wandered off to her study.

It was one of those strange little conversations I have with Mum where nothing has been said, but it's not as if we haven't said anything.

It wasn't until I was washing the last pastry cutter that I realised we hadn't actually invited Ben and Sam to the party. I didn't bother knocking on Ben's watermelon door; I went straight round to Marilyn's. He was there of course. Marilyn invited me in to see how the cot was getting on.

It was just like they were married! Well, how you imagine married might be anyway. Obviously, my own family set-up is pretty odd and tends to involve doing different things in different rooms, sometimes with different people, but I know the theory.

Ben was up in the baby's room, covered in dabs of paint in all the colours of butterflies that were on the cot. If it wasn't for his jeans and shirt, you could almost imagine he was a butterfly, and perhaps he was. A multicoloured, grown-up Ben, emerged from the caterpillar Ben I'd known before.

Marilyn sat down in a corner of the room and picked up her book. She reads everything she can get her hands on, all the time. Not just the kinds of book you'd think she'd read – the ones with moody-looking rebels on the front. No, she reads newspapers and magazines and history books and science books and comics. Today she was reading about some bloke who painted murals in Mexico. I bet she'll ask Ben to paint a wall of the house next.

I wouldn't blame her – Ben's butterflies were fantastic. However vague, irritating and indecisive Ben is, no one could ever pretend he isn't brilliant with a brush. I don't know if he will end up being a painter. Most painters don't seem to be painters all the time. They're usually cleaners or teachers, and I don't think Ben wants to be a cleaner or teacher just so he can be a painter.

It was really calm in the baby's room – partly, I suppose, because the baby wasn't there. They'd put her in her mum's room to keep her away from the paint fumes. How responsible. I would never have thought of that. They suddenly seemed like parents again. There were no obvious signs of flirting. In fact, they weren't even talking, because Marilyn was reading. Nevertheless, I felt that something fishy was going on. Why was Marilyn sitting reading in the same room as Ben anyway, and why was he not objecting?

There was nothing I could do. Well, I could have asked them to tell me exactly how they felt about each other, but I couldn't bring myself to do it. I admit I can be nosy, but did I really want to know? I made an excuse about having to clean out my goldfish – which wasn't a very good excuse, because I haven't got any goldfish.

Chapter Six
The Party's Over

Not eight o'clock yet and only one guest, who was almost in tears.
The party was hardly swinging.

I went round to Sam's feeling relieved that I wouldn't have to deal with any girls, especially as Liz was round at my house planning her Great Escape with Max. I didn't know why they were bothering to go away. They wouldn't see anything except each other's noses, or just blackness if they kissed with their eyes shut.

But if by the time I left Marilyn's I felt chewed up, when I left Sam's I felt as if I was speeding down the alimentary canal with no brakes. Sam was out and his mum told me he'd gone to look for a vital flywheel for his robot. I tried to hide my red cheeks by pretending I had inadvertently put on a thermal vest. I think she believed me, because she gave me some home-made ice-cream to cool me down. I told her to give Sam the message about the party and then ran home, clutching the flywheel in my pocket. I ate all the ice-cream but I still felt hot.

Usually when I feel bad I read my film script and imagine myself directing, acting and giving autographs. Then, to be honest, I have a little play with my toy soldiers. I did all that, but it didn't work. I still felt pants about nicking Sam's flywheel. I told Alex, and we decided I should tell Sam what I'd done when he came over for the party.

We worked all afternoon getting it ready. Finishing off the food, cooling the drinks, choosing the music, setting up the chess game. I also prepared a medieval general knowledge quiz with a special section on you know who, Mr Hood. I even tidied up Max's room, an unpleasant task which involved picking up food, drink, magazines, CDs and, horrifically, Liz's see-through bra. I put it in a clear plastic bag like they do with evidence in crime films.

I didn't mind much when Sam and Ben didn't arrive on the dot of seven. They never arrive on the dot of anything, except the dot of half an hour late. By quarter to eight, though, I was ready to chew up the chess board. Luckily Ben arrived soon after. Not only was I glad to see him, but I won that chess board in a competition and so didn't really want to eat it.

He looked different. I couldn't work out what it was at first, but then I realised: he looked clean. Not that Ben is particularly dirty. He's as clean as me and I'm averaging two and a half baths a week. Tonight he looked a different kind of clean. Scrubbed clean. This was worrying, until I noticed he'd still got paint in his hair. I was relieved, and happy to tease him.

'Are you going to take off and fly round the garden?'

'What do you mean?' he said, his brow furrowing a bit.

'You've got all the butterfly colours in your hair.'

'I know,' he said.

'Can't you get them out?'

'They're not supposed to come out.' He turned away and tried one of Alex's blinis. He clearly liked it, because he swallowed it whole.

'You mean you're going to go to school with paint in your hair?'

'It's not paint.'

'What is it, then?'

He ate another blini. Alex peered at his head.

'Is it dye?'

'Yeah,' he said, so quietly and vaguely that it was almost like he was just breathing out.

'Why have you dyed your hair?'

'I haven't.'

I felt really irritated.

'You just said you had!'

'Did Marilyn do it?' said Alex kindly.

'Yeah,' breathed Ben.

I erupted: 'Why on earth did you let her do that?'

'I wanted her to!' he gasped, and he looked like he was nearly crying.

Not eight o'clock yet and only one guest, who was almost in tears. The party was hardly swinging.

'I think it looks good,' said Alex, smiling.

'Thanks,' said Ben, sniffing. 'They're the same colours as on the cot.'

We ate and drank a bit and then I decided we had to take action about Sam. I rang his house and his mum told me something almost as shocking as Ben's hair: he was at Natalie's!

Without even discussing it, we raced round there. Natalie's house is unusual, because it's part of the organic farm on the edge of town, and because her parents built it, and because it's saving the planet. So you have to get past the goats and pigs and sheep and ducks before you reach the house, which is on the far side of the farm. Then you have to find the door, which is tricky, because her parents have moved it a few times. Then you have to find where everyone is. This ought to be easy, because the house is actually one huge room, but it's divided by these woven twig fences into different-sized living-working-sleeping-eating-playing-giving-birth spaces. Natalie's parents have needed quite a few of those, because they've had six children. After each baby's born, they rearrange the twigs to make a nursery, and bigger bedrooms for the potentially jealous siblings.

The door was open, so we rushed into the house and went racing round, looking for Sam. There were various kids in various bits, and a sheep too: Perhaps it was an orphan that needed bottle-feeding, or maybe it was a new pet – I didn't have time to ask. I found Sam first. He was sitting on the floor in the big playroom, doing his robot. Natalie was tidying up some toys and her brother Ricky was watching Sam. An innocent scene, you might think. Not to me.

'What are you doing here?' I asked him, quite snappily, but I couldn't help it.

'Doing my robot,' he muttered, still fiddling and not looking up.

What was going on? Was this a front? Could he possibly have fallen for Natalie? I didn't want to ask him all these questions in case I gave him an idea that hadn't occurred to him. Also, the real reason was dawning on me, and I was dreading finding out I was right. Ricky put me out of my potential misery, or into it, whichever way you look at it.

'He needed a flywheel, the shops were shut and I've got one,' he said cheerily.

Little did he realise how bad this news was. Of course, I'd known Sam would need the flywheel eventually, but I hadn't known how badly or how soon. I could have let the whole thing go, but Sam meant too much to me. I had to risk everything, in front of all these people.

'I took it,' I said quietly.

Everyone looked at me, even the sheep.

'Took what?' said Ricky innocently, pointing to the flywheel in the robot. 'It's here.'

Sam knew what I meant. He looked up at me and, I think for the first time ever, those soft brown eyes were hard and angry.

'I needed it, Joe. You knew I needed it.'

'I know, and I needed to talk to you. I was sick of you fiddling with that thing!'

'But you know if I've a chance of getting on *Tomorrow's World*—'

'I know,' I shrieked, 'but that's going to take years. I can't wait to talk to you until then!'

Alex put his hand on my arm. I breathed out like a horse after a long race. I felt tired. I walked away from all the metal bits and saw Natalie looking straight at me. She is direct, and I expected her to say something, even tell me off, but she didn't. She just knelt there with a bit of jigsaw in her hand.

The phone rang. No one seemed to want to answer it, but eventually it stopped ringing and Natalie's sister came in.

'It's for you,' she said to Natalie.

'Who is it?' asked Natalie.

'It sounds like Big Bob again.'

'Tell him I'm not in.'

Sam looked up again, not angry this time. He looked straight at Natalie and she looked straight back at him. It suddenly felt like there were too many people in that room.

'Are you coming over to Joe's?' said Ben, gently.

'Yeah, in a while, when I've done this bit,' said Sam.

We walked home along the river. It's wider up at the farm, with warehouses on the banks and barges at the water's edge, all derelict. There was so much we could talk about – what was happening with Sam and Natalie, maybe even what was happening with Natalie and Big Bob – but it was all too complicated and scary, so we didn't talk at all. It started to rain and none of us had hoods. We never do, but I felt wetter than usual.

When we got back the party didn't seem such a good idea any more. I wasn't hungry or thirsty or in the mood for chess. Ben turned the telly on and watched a makeover show. Alex wanted some food, so I went up to the kitchen with him. Mum was hovering about.

'How's the party going?'

'Fine.'

I didn't feel like telling her everything. She'd try to make me feel better and I didn't want that. I felt like feeling bad for a bit longer. She stared madly at the blinis.

'Would you like one?' asked Alex.

'I shouldn't really. Gluten makes me sluggish.'

She had three.

Munching the third while she fiddled with the magnets on the fridge, she said casually, 'Max not around tonight?'

'He's gone away with Liz, hasn't he?' I said, thinking she must have forgotten.

'He's what?' she said, with her mouth open and a blob of sour cream stuck to the corner of it.

I told her again, in case she hadn't heard: 'He's gone away with Liz.'

This time she froze, except for the blob of sour cream, which fell to the floor, and her eyes, which were dilating wildly.

'I'm going to have to talk to Dad!' she said, with a horrified look, and she rushed out of the room and down the stairs.

I didn't know which was worse for her: Max and Liz going away or talking to Dad. We listened to her boots clanking down to Dad's flat, then low voices, then her boots and Dad's boots clanking back up. Funnily enough, they wear the same boots. Not the same pair, obviously, but the same style. They both want the other one to change but they're too stubborn to do it themselves.

We all congregated in Max's room.

'How do you know they've gone away?' asked Dad, calmly but firmly.

'I thought you knew!' I said defensively.

'That wasn't what I asked you.'

'He told me.'

Mum and Dad went Very Serious. Very Serious applies to situations like Getting Detention (always Max, actually), Borrowing Money without Asking, and Fighting with Blood on the Carpet. It's not the carpet, it's the drawing blood, though Mum in particular gets quite upset about the carpet too.

Alex and I went very quiet. Ben was asleep (too much late-night painting, obviously). Mum rang Max's mobile but it was turned off. Dad announced he was going to ring the police. Mum made him a cup of coffee. It was weird, seeing them act like parents who get on.

*

Sam didn't turn up to the party and anyway it wasn't really a party any more. Alex and I woke up Ben and made sure he got home. When we got back to the house Max and Liz were there. They seemed surprisingly relaxed. Relaxed enough to you-know-what.

'What did Dad say?' I asked, with great concern.

'I don't know,' he said, a bit irritated at being interrupted. 'Is he in?'

'He's ringing the police about you!' I exclaimed.

This did make him stop kissing and sit up. I must remember that for the future.

'Why?'

'Because you said you were going away together!'

'We changed our minds. We've just been to the cinema.'

Alex put his hand on my arm for the second time that evening. I quite wanted today to be over but I knew that, unfortunately, there was a bit more to come.

I told Mum and Mum told Dad, just before he started wasting police time. I asked if Alex could stay a bit longer and we all sat in Max's room, which is the only neutral room big enough for us all to be in at the same time.

Dad grilled Max in the way that even easygoing dads do when you've done something wrong. Except that Max hadn't done anything wrong: he'd just gone to the cinema with Liz, which he's allowed to do. Yes, they were thinking of going away somewhere, but they didn't because of the rain. Can you believe it!

Dad couldn't really grill Max for something he was only thinking of doing. Anyway, now he knew he couldn't go away with his girlfriend, he probably wouldn't. Dad looked at a bit of a loss for someone to grill, so I told him he might as well grill me. I was the one who'd got everything wrong: I'd told Mum about Max's plan which resulted in Mum having to talk to Dad, Dad having to ring the police and Max being furious with me. This would probably last days and involve all kinds of torment. Quite an achievement for one small Saturday night.

Mum suggested we all had an early night. I felt totally empty, and full up at the same time. Alex sat quietly next to me and I suddenly wanted him to stay the night. I asked Mum if he could, pretty sure she'd say no. Luckily, parents are completely unpredictable and she said yes.

We went down to my room and he suddenly said, 'I can't stay.'

'Why not?'

'I just can't.'

'Why didn't you say so before, when I asked Mum?'

'I was embarrassed.'

'Embarrassed! I've had one of the most embarrassing evenings of my life and now you're saying you're embarrassed just because you can't stay for a sleepover!'

'I'm sorry, Joe. There's a reason I can't stay. I will explain.'

'Go on, then.'

'I can't explain now.'

'Why not?'

'It's too complicated.'

'Is it something about me?'

'No, it's something about me.'

'Have you got smelly feet?'

He laughed.

'No. I've really got to go.'

Reluctantly, I asked Dad to give him a lift back up to the heath. I watched them go from my window. It was still raining and he still didn't have a hood. Just before he got in the car, he picked at his jumper with his fingers, fluffing it up and out. I realised he does that quite a lot. Must be a nervous habit. Funny boy. I watched Dad's car turn the corner and felt sad that it was only a week until the circus moved on.

Chapter Seven

The Film

*'I think we should make my film,' I called over to Alex, who was now
sitting in a ruined window frame, fiddling with his jumper,
like he does.*

When I woke up on Sunday morning I spent a long time
staring at Heath Ledger. He's got long legs, dark eyes, curly
hair and he's a film star. So we're pretty similar, apart from
the last bit. So far, anyway. I am planning to be a film star,
but as I want to be a director, writer and producer as well,
I'm not sure when I'll fit the film star bit in. I ought to do
the film star bit first, I suppose, because looks go off, don't
they? My dad was very handsome once, but now he's got
hairs growing out of his ears and that spoils the effect. I tell
him when I see one and he cuts it off, but there's always a
danger that it could have sprouted a few hours before I
notice it.

The other problem with being a film star is that you get
lots of girls wanting to go out with you, or at the very least
wanting to stick your photo on their bedroom wall. That's

what I've done with Heath Ledger, although of course I'm not a girl, and it's not on the wall, it's on the ceiling. I've got this platform bed which my dad built for me. It's great, because there's loads of room underneath for my desk, my clothes and all my catapults. The flip side is that there's not a lot of room between me and the ceiling. Also, I've had the bed for a while and I must have got thicker (chest not brain), so when I look at Heath Ledger I nearly go cross-eyed.

Mum says he's really handsome. She has got to this really sad stage where she comes along to teen movies pretending that she wants to keep up with my interests but really because she fancies all the handsome young film stars. That's another difference between Heath and me. I may have some of the same attributes, but they don't add up. He looks handsome; I look weird. Mum disagrees and thinks I'm just as handsome as him, but that's another truly sad thing about mothers: they all think their children are gorgeous. I suppose someone has to, even if they're wrong.

I reached behind Heath's back and got out my notebook. I had decided to keep a record of the club's activities and I didn't want anyone else to read it, so it was hidden between the poster and the ceiling. I like having secrets – it makes me feel deep. I wrote:

THE BOYS' CLUB
Report of activities so far

Successful events
1) Midnight thrash

Not so successful
1) Ben is spending a lot of time with a G.I.R.L.
2) Sam has gone mad on his robot, which resulted in him going to the house of a G.I.R.L.
3) Sam is furious with me for putting one of his flywheels in my pocket (I suppose that's stealing).
4) Max is *still* going out with Liz. It's been 34 days now. Surely it must end soon?

I read over the list and all in all I wasn't ecstatic. I could have added some more items to the 'successful' list, like '2) The blinis tasted good,' but I knew that would be cheating. I sighed heavily, even though I wasn't in a film and there was no one to hear. Something had to be done. I was chairman of this club – well, no one had asked me to be and we hadn't had a vote, but it felt right – and I had to make it work.

Mum popped in, so I quickly hid the notebook back under the poster. She came right over to my bed and leant her head back and peered at the ceiling. I thought maybe she'd seen the secret notebook and would read it the next time she dusted my room, in a year or two. Then I realised she was trying to look at Heath. I've got loads of other posters in my room but she always looks at that one.

'You should get one for your ceiling,' I said helpfully.

'Don't be ridiculous!' she said, as if I had suggested she wear her bra on her head. 'I've got George Clooney on my ceiling.'

'Oh, yeah' I said, remembering the poster she'd bought me to give her for Christmas.

'If only he'd fall off and land on top of me,' she said dreamily.

'But then you wouldn't be able to look at the poster,' I pointed out.

'I don't think I'd mind about that,' she said, so dreamily, I thought she was going to shut her eyes and nod off.

'Did you come in here to regress?'

'No!' she said, snapping out of it and back into her life as a mum and natural childbirth expert. 'I've come to see if you want to invite someone to lunch. We're having roast.' To many, a roast would mean a sizzling lump of dead animal. To us it means a selection of root and Mediterranean vegetables, with a bit of pesto if we're feeling festive. I like winding Mum up by telling her my childhood's been deprived of animal fat, but I actually really like my veg. Luckily no one at school knows except Ben and Sam.

Usually I would have invited Ben or Sam, or if I couldn't decide which of them, both of them. Mum doesn't mind peeling more parsnips. Today I didn't feel right about inviting either of them, and I didn't feel right about not feeling right. As two not-feeling-rights don't make a feeling-right, I decided to ring Alex instead.

That's not so simple. His family live in a caravan, they only have a mobile and most of his family don't speak much English, so when they answer you get a splurge of Slavic sounds coming at you. At first, I tried, 'It's Joe here, could I speak to Alex, please?' but that got me nowhere, except put through to the circus box office. Now I just say, 'Alex-Alex-Alex,' like an SOS call, and he gets put on straight away. Or five minutes later if he's up on the tightrope. They once handed the phone to him while he was *on* the tightrope. He was OK about it, but I couldn't relax.

He couldn't come to lunch because he had to work on the matinée show, so I suggested we meet at the castle later on. He'd never been, and as we'd known each other for fourteen days and he was now one of my three joint best friends, I felt he should see my favourite place.

I waited in front of the ticket office, just over the

drawbridge. The usual stream of ladies in macs trundled over. I don't really know why they come. I think it's to smell the flowers and eat the flapjacks. I don't reckon they imagine full medieval battles, like I do.

For a moment I thought I was about to witness one. A white mare came storming towards me. It clattered over the drawbridge and I stood aside, expecting it to go into the ticket office and ask for the equine discount. Instead, it came to a stop right in front of me and did one of those snorty breaths that spray you with horse snot. I was about to complain to the rider when I looked up and saw it was Alex.

'My liege,' quoth I, 'hast thou come to do justice for the common man?'

'Not really,' said Alex. 'I've come to give Monika some exercise.' He swung his leg over the saddle and leapt off. 'She is stuck in that tent all week with a Brazilian spinning on her back. I thought it would be nice for her to have some fresh air.'

Although the castle would have been packed with horses in the 1550s, we weren't actually allowed to take Monika in. Alex tied her to the drawbridge and we went for a walk around the moat, while she looked down on us from above.

I was quite quiet. Compared to how I usually am, I was extremely quiet, so compared to people who don't talk much, I was silent. Alex realised something was wrong. Mind you, I was doing quite a lot of sighing as well, but he is very sensitive nevertheless.

'Is it the club?' he asked. He's pretty intuitive too.

'Yes,' I said. 'It's not going very well.'

'Is it because of me?' he asked.

'No!' I exclaimed. 'It's the others. Ben's spending all this time with Marilyn and Sam's been round at Natalie's house. I know that was for a flywheel, but you can never tell. One flywheel could lead to another, and another, and then he'll stay for a drink and next thing you know they'll be an item. A kissing item.'

'This hasn't happened yet,' Alex said encouragingly.

'No, but it might,' I said discouragingly.

'But it hasn't.'

'But it might.'

I was getting stuck again. I do. I once spent three days trying to work out how I could buy a replica of Bodiam Castle, complete with two armies and a siege tower, for 95p. This was how much I had in my money box. The price on the castle was £54.75. Eventually Dad suggested I buy one soldier and save for the rest. By the time I'd saved some more money, I'd moved on to the Napoleonic era and desperately wanted some Prussians. At least that got me out of the castle fix.

'I think you're thinking too much,' said Alex, skimming a stone over the moat. Five bounces. Not bad. 'You're thinking too much about *not* seeing girls and you've forgotten to enjoy seeing the boys.'

'That's because I haven't seen them much recently.'

'Exactly.'

'But I tried having a party and look where that got me. Full of blinis and in trouble.'

'Maybe a party wasn't right. Maybe it was trying to do something you do with girls, but without girls. Maybe you should do something you do with boys and do it with boys.'

Boy, was this boy on the ball, I thought. He was like one of those psychological experts you see on TV talk shows who sort out people's physical, emotional and financial problems in one sentence like, 'You have to believe in yourself.'

Then he wandered away from me and did a series of amazing gymnastic leaps over a pile of ruined stones. Like Errol Flynn. I couldn't believe it. Not only had he told me I needed to do something, he'd shown me what it was too!

My film! *Robin Hood: The Teenage Years*. I wrote it a year ago and it's still not been made. I put it in for a film competition and it didn't win. I think they didn't understand it. It's not like all the other Robin Hood films in that

Robin Hood isn't this brilliant handsome fighter who rids the Midlands of evil and then settles down with Maid Marian. I've written about the years *before* he turned into Errol Flynn or Kevin Costner, when he was a bit less handsome and confident. I've thought a lot about super-heroes and how they may not have been born superheroes but slowly became them after they'd got through adolescence. You can't flatten Mr Freeze if you've got spots. You can't take on the Joker if you've got a funny little fuzzy moustache.

As I see it, Robin Hood was born quite shy, the kind of boy who had small birthday parties and never wanted swimming lessons. He sucked his thumb until he was six and bit his nails until he was ten. Then he slowly developed through his teenage years, with the help of a few good friends, into a total hero. My film is set when he's about twelve and he's quite depressed. That might sound a bit boring, but it's got lots of fantasy sequences, where he's imagining what he's like when he's older. Or it could be that we're actually seeing what he becomes when he's older. It could be either. That's why the film's so deep. But I think maybe it's too deep, and so the competition judges didn't understand it and that's why I didn't win. It might also have been because of my spelling.

'I think we should make my film,' I called over to Alex,

who was now sitting in a ruined window frame, fiddling with his jumper, like he does.

'Yeah, good idea,' he said, as if it was mine, but actually he had given it to me.

'I think you should be Robin Hood,' I said.

He looked a bit cross.

'Why?'

I meant to say, 'Because you're good at acrobatics,' but for some reason I said something completely different. 'Because you're handsome.'

'That's why you should do it,' he said quickly.

'You think Robin Hood wasn't a looker?' I asked.

'I think he was. That's why you should do it, because you are.'

He looked straight at me. He was sitting in the window frame and I was standing on the stones. It was one of those terrible moments that I find pop up much too often these days. You can be wandering along quite happily and then, *whoops!*, you fall down a huge gaping manhole full of embarrassment and fear right bang in the middle of your path.

Boys of twelve don't tell each other they're handsome! Why did we do that? Sam, Ben and I, we chug along like trains on parallel tracks, quite happy together most of the time and heading roughly in the same direction. With

Alex, it's better, and worse, than that. It's like going on a huge ocean voyage. Sometimes it's calm and the air is still, and we could be dancing on the deck (not with each other of course), and sometimes it's as if there's a terrible storm and the ship is going down and me with it.

He was still looking at me. Those deep, dark eyes again. The ship was rocking and rolling. Then he suddenly set things right. He smiled, climbed out of the palace window and hopped down the stones and on to the grass.

'Let's choose the locations!' he called without looking back at me.

I ran after him. We were OK again. The weird moment had passed and we were two ordinary boys planning our award-winning film.

Chapter Eight

Who Plays Whom?

'If you're Marian, and I'm John, and he's Robin Hood, I'm off.'

The first thing to sort out was who was going to play whom. I've just learnt 'whom' in English. Sounds nutty, doesn't it?

I didn't want to go back to the delicate question of who should play Robin Hood. I just assumed it was going to be me. I'm not that like him really, but it'd be a challenge for my acting skills. I'd have to act handsome. I'd always seen Ben as Little John, and I asked Alex to be Will Scarlet. He's a really good fighter in my film, but only in the dream sequences, so that means it's not real fighting, which is OK, I think. Alex could do some great stunts.

Friar Tuck was a problem. The obvious person to play him was Sam, because, to be honest, he does have a bit of a belly, but that's also the reason why I couldn't ask him. I decided to modernise the part and make him Friar Truck, who's the Merry Men's mechanic and isn't necessarily tubby. Sam could play that part very well.

Then there was the tricky question of Maid Marian. I couldn't really do without her. I mean I could, but I don't think Robin in the film could. She's not in it much; she's just in the dream sequences, and even then she's a bit of a blur, but I didn't think I could get away with a boy in a wig doing it. I'd have to ask a girl. Of course, there was a danger that if I made the film with a girl I'd have to talk to her and that might lead to all sorts of terrible actions that would contravene the Boys' Club rules. I was prepared to take that risk. I was doing pretty well so far, especially compared to Ben and Sam. I felt I could make a film with Kylie Minogue and not be tempted.

Who should I ask? I needed someone who was good at acting, and sort of attractive, and would say yes. I pretended that I had to think about this for a long time, but it was actually really obvious who it should be: Marilyn. She was in our Year Six production of *Chitty Chitty Bang Bang* and she made a great Truly Scrumptious.

I was going to ask Ben if he minded me asking her. I didn't know why he would mind. They weren't going out or anything, were they? However, events conspired against my plan.

The next morning felt like any Monday morning at school. The usual yawn-fest. Then something different happened. Mr Carson came in, but not with his usual scurry. He strode manfully to the desk and he looked us in the eye.

'Ben,' he said, 'what has happened to your hair?'

'I've dyed it,' said Ben, smiling, and with a glance at Marilyn.

'Then would you please go home and undye it,' said Mr Carson.

We all stared. This was not the Mr Carson we'd come to know and liked to tease.

Ben spoke for us all when he asked, 'Are you OK, sir? You've gone all tough.'

'I'm not tough, Ben. I'm assertive. I've been on a course.'

Not courses again. Whenever our teachers go on courses, they come back with a new personality. Mr Dodds was a real laugh until he went on a course about 'Authority in the Classroom'. He's not much fun now.

'I'll do something about it tonight.'

'Now, please, Ben. Dyed hair is not acceptable in this school.'

'But look at Marilyn's. Hers is like a tropical rainforest!'

We all looked at Marilyn's hair. Ben was right. She had parrots and orchids today.

'It's not dyed, Ben. Now, would you please go and sort your hair out.'

84

Ben got up and left. I felt sick. Ben had never been thrown out of anything, except the toddler group, and that was because he bit Sam. Fair enough. I glared at Mr Carson, but he didn't notice. He was too busy asking us to face the front. Despite his new-found assertiveness, that took all morning.

At break I was all over the place. It didn't *look* like I was all over the place, but more like I'd developed a sudden fascination with floors. I stood by the school phone, staring at the tiles, which I can report have wispy bits of white and red on a grey background, just like our school tie. Well, my school tie. It's meant to be grey, but I've spilt toothpaste and ketchup down it and it won't come out. This annoys Mum so much she's threatened to put me up for adoption, even at this late stage. I reckon it looks quite good and I'm going to suggest it to the school council as the official tie design. Then everyone could spill food down their shirt and the result would be a) happier kids and b) me in less trouble.

I got stuck because I didn't know what to do and all my thoughts were churning round me like sugar in a candy-floss machine. I find the more I struggle on the inside the more stuck I get on the outside. I once spent two hours sitting on my bed deciding what castle I wanted for Christmas. Dad seriously thought I'd spilt superglue on the duvet.

Here's a small selection of my thoughts. Should I ring

Ben and talk to him about his hair? Should I ask him what he thought about me asking Marilyn to be in the film, or did that make it seem like it would be a problem, which would then give him the idea it *was* a problem? Should I just go straight and ask Marilyn to be in the film? How scary would that be? Would I have time to ask Marilyn *and* buy a bun, bearing in mind I'd now spent half of break thinking about all this?

It was my great good luck that this cycle of useless rumination was broken by Marilyn herself.

'Hi, Joe.'

'Hi.' There was a long pause while I decided what to say next and then it just popped out: 'Marilyn.'

It didn't seem as if this conversation was going to flow.

'Have you got Ben's phone number?'

'Yes,' I said, with great certainty. Things were picking up. This talking to girls wasn't as bad as I'd thought. Maybe I'd try it again sometime.

'Are you going to tell me what it is?'

I was in trouble again. Not only had I taken a ridiculously long time to answer, but I realised I'd forgotten Ben's phone number. I always go round when I want to talk to him, because he's only a few doors away. Sometimes I even shout over the garden walls if it's something simple, like, 'Lend us a fiver.'

Under huge emotional, social and numerical pressure, I remembered it, and gave it to Marilyn. Then, after a pathetically slow start to this conversation, it picked up and gained an alarming speed.

'I thought I'd ring him and see if he's all right about his hair,' she said.

'Yes, I will too,' I said.

'I think Mr Carson was way out of order,' she said.

'Yeah,' I said. 'Do you want to be in my film?'

'What film's that, then?'

'*Robin Hood: The Teenage Years*. You could be Maid Marian.'

'OK, then.'

That was it. Probably the longest conversation I'd had with a woman, apart from my mum and, in earlier years, the lollipop lady. A vast exchange of information and ideas. Marilyn went off down the corridor, taking her layers of clothes (she even manages to layer school uniform) and her rainforest hair with her. Now that the conversation was over I suddenly realised I hadn't arranged to meet up and plan the filming. I took immediate action and ran after Marilyn, risking the explosion of a school rumour that I was after her. Well, I was, but not in that way. I had to build on the easy communication we'd enjoyed and casually asked her if she could come round to my house after school, to talk about the film.

She said yes, so that was a triumph. I decided I'd ring Ben later because the bell went for the end of break. Who knows what punishment for being late the new tough Mr Carson might inflict. It would certainly be stronger than his old one, which was writing a list of your top ten favourite films.

As I was going back upstairs, I saw Natalie right down at the end of the corridor. Nothing so strange about that. I see her all the time at school. Sometimes I even say hello. But Big Bob was standing opposite her and between them was a brightly wrapped parcel that looked suspiciously like a present. Natalie pushed it away, back towards Bob, and then ran down the corridor. I dived into the classroom, uncomfortable with what I'd seen.

At dinner-time, I ran the Friar Truck idea past Sam. It didn't go too well.

'Is he the fat bloke?'

'Um, he is. I mean, he can be traditionally, but not necessarily.'

'Is that why you asked me to be him?' he said, looking down at his belly, which honestly comes out only just a tiny bit over his trousers.

'No!' I exclaimed about the whole Friar Truck body-image issue. 'Anyway, he's Friar *Truck*. He's the mechanic.'

'They didn't need mechanics in the Middle Ages.'

I hadn't thought of that. I had to improvise.

'But they had carts! And their weapons must have needed mending sometimes. That's sort of mechanical.'

Sam put his hands in his pockets and fiddled with the bits and pieces that were in there. This is always an indication that he's thinking, or hungry.

'Yeah, I'll do it.'

I was really pleased, and relieved. I now knew something of how top directors feel when they're casting a film. Trying to decide between Matt Dillon and Ben Affleck. In my case, I just had Sam, but it hadn't been easy and it wasn't over.

'As long as I don't have to act.'

'No, of course not!' I said, fibbing. 'Just be yourself.'

'You mean fat?'

'No!' I said, almost annoyed.

I bet they don't get these problems in Hollywood. Of course they don't, because they don't have anyone a gram overweight. This is why my film is going to be so great, because it's about real people with real spots.

Marilyn doesn't have any spots, actually, but Pom-Pom does. I'm told they're called milk spots. I know this because Marilyn brought the baby to the meeting. Their mum had been recording half the night and now had to sleep three-quarters of the day. I wasn't too pleased: the baby might cry and interrupt the flow. Marilyn suggested we make the most of it and put the baby in the film. Marian could have a mum with a baby Marian has to look after. Art mirroring life and all that. I'm not so sure. I'd prefer art to be in a sealed box with a big label saying: 'This isn't about me.'

The weirdest thing was Alex. He was really into the baby. He asked to hold her and told Marian he had a niece with a similar name, but in Polish it sounded more like a sneeze. When I came into the room with the drinks and snacks, it was like he suddenly remembered to be different. He dumped the baby on Marilyn's knee and started talking about the football results, but the season was over and there weren't any. How weird is that?

To my surprise, Sam didn't bring any tools or materials. I couldn't believe it. Ever since I've known him he's had something in his hand, even if it was only his other hand, so he could build a tower with his fingers. I was about to comment, but then he started tucking into the biscuits, not eating them but making a shape on the table. In an uncharacteristic fit of domestic awareness, I realised the table was going to get all crumby and asked him to stop.

'Can I have some paper, then?'

'We're here to read, not write,' I reminded him.

'I know, but I've got some ideas I've got to get down.'

'I've already written the script.'

'They're not for the script, they're for Natalie's pigsty.'

Sam has an odd way of telling me things. Like giving me a bar of fudge and then telling me he's going to Edinburgh for the whole of the summer holidays and they make fudge there. Now it seems that Natalie said her parents were so impressed with Sam's skills, they want him to design a pigsty for the farm. A great building opportunity for Sam; a potential total and utter stinking disaster for the Boys' Club. This project could involve acres of time spent with Natalie. A romantic liaison might be unavoidable. Love is all about time, I think. My parents met on a six-week archaeological dig in Wales. I wonder if they'd have fallen in love if they'd met at some traffic lights.

I couldn't worry about Sam and Natalie, because Ben arrived and then I really had something to worry about. For a start, he looked strange. He'd taken the dye out of his hair and it was all dry and frizzy. Then he acted strange.

He stared and stared at Marilyn and said flatly, as if his voice was staring too, 'Why are you here?'

'I'm Maid Marian.'

'Not if I'm Little John.'

'It's OK, Ben, I'm Robin Hood,' I said helpfully.

Perhaps he'd got confused and thought Little John fell

for Marian. Perhaps he was thinking about the club rules. At that point, however, I was unable to delve into his thoughts.

'Exactly,' he said, less flatly. More with a considerable hillock of anger. 'If you're Marian, and I'm John, and he's Robin Hood, I'm off.'

And he left. We were as silent as sleeping spiders. The read-through was over before it had begun. And so, I suspected, was the film.

Chapter Nine

People Going Out

'People going out are never happy. They're always sighing and fiddling with their hair.'

We all stayed quiet, except for the baby, who started crying. Marilyn used this as an excuse to go, because I'm sure she wanted to go and talk to Ben. I did too, but I also didn't. I knew we'd have one of those conversations where we both say, 'But I thought you thought . . .' lots of times. They're very tiring, and I already felt tired. Tired of trying to make everything happen. Sometimes I felt like the more I tried the more things went wrong. Maybe I should copy Sam and spend more time with my hands in my pockets.

Alex cleared away the few remaining biscuits and I picked up the cans, crushing them – ready for recycling, and also because I was upset. Sam suddenly stood up.

'Can I have some more paper?'

'Haven't you got any at home?' I asked, because I was surprised, not mean.

'I've got to go down to the farm to take some measurements.'

I found him some paper and could so easily have simply given it to him, then said goodbye, but out popped, 'Are you doing this because of Natalie?'

'Who?'

'Nothing.'

He went, and Alex and I flopped on the sofa like an old couple. I sighed. I was hoping Alex would cheer me up. Maybe I should have asked him to, instead of letting him say what he wanted.

'Do you think everyone is falling in love?'

'I don't know,' I said, a bit grumpily.

'What if they do?'

'Then there's nothing I can do about it,' I said morosely.

'Why does all this make you so sad?'

'Because they're my friends! I want them to be happy.'

'What if they're happy going out with Marilyn and Natalie?'

'How could they be?' I retorted. 'People going out are never happy. They're always sighing and fiddling with their hair.'

'Sounds like you, and you're not going out with anyone.'

'Whose side are you on?'

He did a few scary stretches, like putting his leg over

his head. Was this to impress me or because he felt uncomfortable? I'd feel highly uncomfortable, doing the stretches.

'Why aren't we acting like everyone else our age?'

'Because we're more mature,' I told him.

'Maybe it's because we're more scared.'

'I'm not scared!'

'Why don't you fall for a girl, then?'

'Why don't you?'

He flicked right over the end of the sofa.

'I'm only here until Saturday. Doesn't seem worth it.'

'That's an excuse. Is there someone you like?'

He flicked back and nearly landed in my lap.

'Sorry,' he said. 'Yes, there is.'

'Who?'

'Nothing's going to happen, so there's no point saying.'

'Course there is. I am chairman of the club and I demand that you tell me!'

'No!'

He jumped away from me onto the armchair. Despite the fragility of the table, I leapt on it and lunged at him. The chair swivelled round, with us both in it, half tickling, half fighting, both laughing. I'm not very strong, but Alex wasn't as strong as I thought he was. I'd soon got him pinned down.

'Get off!' he yelled at me.

His eyes were really burning. Furious and upset. He looked like he was going to cry again. I let go of him and went back to the sofa. He picked at his jumper, pulling it away from him like it was on fire.

'Are you OK?' I asked, as gently as I could.

'Yeah,' he said. 'Let's not talk about that again.'

Although Alex and I had decided not to talk about girls, I decided that Ben, Sam and I needed to. I got to school early the next day so I could catch them before we went in. It's much better talking to people before school. By the time we've had a couple of lessons we're all dusty and crabby and don't make sense.

I couldn't see Ben, but Marilyn was at the other side of the playground, with her usual rainforest hair, though oddly enough she wasn't wearing her usual layers. I went over, but when I got close she turned round and I was as shocked as when I found hair under my arms. It was Ben! Ben with Marilyn's hair! Well, not literally Marilyn's hair, but his hair done like Marilyn's! With all the flowers and clips. I asked the obvious question.

'What have you done that for?'

'For Mr Carson.'

'He didn't ask you to.'

'No, but he said Marilyn's hair was OK. So mine must be OK too.'

I never ever thought I'd say this: I wanted to talk to Ben about his hair. But I didn't have time. We had to have an emergency club meeting and it was ten to nine. I looked urgently round the playground for Sam. At first I couldn't see him, because he wasn't in the middle with the boys. Then I saw him in the danger zone: at the edge, with the girls. I think they should change the markings in the playground, or maybe add some. As well as football and netball, we should have some extra red lines, to indicate the girls' zone. They could even mark it out with lines in the shape of red lips.

Something in me must have known Sam had strayed, because my gaze flitted over to the girls' zone and, sure enough, he was there. Talking to Natalie. He had some of his drawings in his hand, so they were probably talking about the pigsty. There was still hope. Apparently, though, you can be talking about something quite normal but really you're falling in love. Mum told me that when she was on the dig where she met Dad, they talked about flint for hours and afterwards she knew she was going to have his children. At first I thought she meant that talking about flint made you pregnant, but I know better now.

I was about to take that dangerous step into the girls' zone in order to retrieve Sam when I saw something that left me with my leg in the air over that invisible boundary: Big Bob was lumbering over to Natalie and Sam. He didn't do that polite thing of waiting for a gap in the conversation. My parents are always telling me to do that, but as they don't talk to each other there *are* no gaps.

He walked straight up to Natalie. He didn't actually push Sam out of the way, but Sam did wobble a bit, like a nearly knocked-off coconut on a shy. Big Bob said something, and of course I couldn't hear what it was, but I bet he wasn't asking if he could help her with her homework. At least he's not bothering with Sam, I thought.

Wishful thinking.

He grabbed Sam's drawing and stared at it very close up. OK, so he didn't tear it to pieces, but he was probably just deciding whether to tear it up now or later.

We couldn't have the meeting all that day because Ben got sent home again, because of his hair again. He made a really brave attempt to defend a boy's right to wear stuff in his hair, but Mr Carson wouldn't yield. He must have some kind of information pack from this course he's been on. I think he reads it every night to stay tough.

Marilyn walked out as well, in solidarity, and came

back with her hair empty of wildlife. She looked quite different without all the colour and activity up there. She was pale, but just as beautiful.

I went round to Ben's after school. He was drawing butterflies again, but this time they were on a long strip of paper, a bit like loo roll though not loo roll, of course. If he'd been decorating loo roll I'd have been seriously worried. Although I did see a bit on the local news about a man who painted loo rolls and had an exhibition of them in an art gallery. Seems a bit of a waste to me, but then maybe it meant his loo was full of really great paintings.

I guessed it was a border for the baby's room, but I didn't ask. I could have told him it was really brilliant, which it was, but this was not a time for fluffy, flattering, friendly talk. It was time to be tough.

'Are you going out with Marilyn?'

'No.'

'Are you going to go out with Marilyn?'

'I don't know.'

'Do you want to go out with Marilyn?'

'Pass me that blue pen.'

What kind of answer was that? A clear deflection. It's like when I ask Mum about her and Dad and she starts talking about *her* parents. What have they got to do with it? Lots, apparently, because everything's connected, Mum says. So maybe blue pens have got something to do with Marilyn. Yes, they have! I've just remembered. She used to wear them twisted up in her hair.

'So you're thinking about going out with her?'

'Yes.'

Aha! A clear confession! But then he spoilt it.

'And you think about going out with Britney Spears.'

Not so clear. I decided to say what I had to say. It was my duty as chairman of the club.

'Ben, may I remind you that the one and only rule of the Boys' Club, of which I believe you are still a member, is that we have nothing to do with girls. *You*, if I may say, are in serious danger of having something to do with girls. With *a* girl. With Marilyn. In fact, of having rather a lot to do with a girl. With Marilyn.'

He carried on drawing. Was I making an impression? I built on my theme.

'May I remind you of the dangers? General soppiness, loss of interest in food and football—'

'Oh, grow up, Joe,' Ben said, under his breath, but not so under his breath that I didn't hear. I was outraged.

'I have grown up! Two inches in the last six months.'

'Stop making excuses. I know you're saying all this because you've fallen for her.'

He looked up from his drawing. He didn't look worried any more. He looked clear and strong and a bit scary.

'I haven't!' I blurted.

'Course you have. Why else would you make her Maid Marian and you Robin Hood? I've read the script. I know there's a kiss.'

'But it's in a dream sequence! It's all blurry! We don't really have to do it!'

I felt desperate. He got up and went downstairs. I followed him, clattering on the stripped, stained and stencilled stairs.

'I'm going out!' he shouted, rather obviously, to his mum.

He marched down the stairs. I followed him. He marched out of the front door. I followed him. He marched down the street. I followed him. We walked. We walked and walked and walked. We didn't really know where we were going, but we knew we had to be on the go. We went round and round the block, and then, without saying anything, he went back inside his house and I went inside mine.

When I got up to the middle floor, I heard sniffling. Must be *Titanic* on TV, I thought. Liz is going for the school record for crying genuine tears at it. She's up to 103 times and is in with a chance.

'Joe,' Max called quietly. He obviously wanted me to be second witness. The rules are very tough.

I went in. He was on his own. The TV was off. He had his head in the pillow.

'Can we have a chat?' he mumbled.

A chat! Max had never wanted a chat before. A fight, a fiver, a bit of my cake, but a chat! I sat on his bed, a bit next to him, but not too close, and I stared at his CDs, wondering if he'd ever let me borrow one.

'Liz and I have split up,' he moaned, and started crying again.

Chapter Ten

Big Bob

'We waited in the dark. We ate all the food. I felt a bit queasy,
partly from fear, partly because all the food was cake.'

Max and I don't talk. Of course he *says* things to me. He says things like 'Shut up!' when I'm saying things to him, with the result that we don't talk. Sometimes we can talk in parallel, like if we're both watching TV we can face the same way and make little comments, like tiny drops in separate oceans, but they don't amount to much, they don't ripple out to create anything amounting to a conversation.

Now he talked. Talked and talked and talked. Words spilling out of him, making up for the years of silence. I always thought Max's sharp edges held the soft stuff in. His soppy, raw feelings, the kind that are always popping out of me. Now he couldn't hold it in. His sadness oozed out of him in hot tears, like soft mortar slithering out of a brick wall.

'She just left. She got up and left without saying why!'

He sounded a bit like a bad song but I didn't say anything. I'd leave that for another day, when he was feeling better and I could tease him.

'Why didn't you go after her?' I asked, aware that this was an obvious question, but it was obviously what he should have done.

'I tried, but she ran into The Warren and I lost her.'

The Warren is our local shopping centre. It's always packed with hand-holding couples who walk slowly and soppily, looking at what they've bought, or kissing, or, if it's earrings, doing both at once.

'Did you have a row?' I asked.

I wasn't really that interested but I thought I had to say something. He must have known if he'd had a row and I didn't really want to know. Why did I ask him something he knew and I didn't want to know? It felt so weird, sitting there talking to Max about his emotions. I could have felt flattered that he wanted to talk to me, but I knew he didn't. At that moment he'd have talked to anyone, whether it was Oprah Winfrey or the postman.

'Not really. She wanted to go shopping and I wanted to go to the park.'

I knew why he wanted to go there. So they could kiss without the very real danger of Mum bursting in and asking if Liz likes falafel.

'Why don't you ring her?'

'She told me not to.'

He started crying again. It was like seeing a giant cry. This was Max, who can do keepy-up to twenty, who knows what an aye-aye is, who can do an ace Ali G impression. This was gigantic Max, broken by Liz.

My future became clear. Not in terms of the job I'd have or the car I'd buy, but in terms of the next half-hour. I knew that I would go round to Sam's house and ask Liz what was going on. I would do this despite the fact that Max had sat on me, broken my Lego and laughed at me when I wasn't joking. I would do this despite the fact that Liz was a girl and, until very recently, Max's girlfriend, and therefore out of my preferred orbit. Why would I do this? Perhaps it was because Max once got a book he thought I'd like out of the library for me.

I wasn't exactly delighted at the prospect of talking to Liz, but there *was* the consolation of being offered some cake. Today it was double chocolate, and I had a double helping. I'd have been quite happy to eat it and go straight home, maybe with another piece wrapped in tinfoil, like in a party bag, but I knew I had to go up and face the music, and Liz.

The music was loud, and Liz was also watching TV and

listening to her Discman with one earpiece. Perhaps she was trying to fill up her head so Max got squeezed out. She probably wouldn't want to see me, because I might remind her of him. Although, as I said, we don't look alike, we might smell the same.

I stood in front of her and waved. To my amazement, she switched off the TV and the music system. She kept the Discman on, but I was quite flattered she had put one whole ear at my disposal.

I hovered about, waiting for something to come out of my mouth. She looked straight at me. She really has got great eyes. I can see why Max wants to swim in them. Maybe.

'Max needs to know why you don't want to go out with him.' I said. Quite a good start, I thought.

'Oh. Because—' she said, and then she stopped and shrugged, with almost all her body.

Was that the reason? 'Because?' Was this some new over-fourteens code? I waited for a bit, but she didn't say anything more. She didn't even do a shrug, of any size. I started to leave.

'He wouldn't come shopping,' she suddenly said.

'Oh,' I said, as if I understood, but really I was buying time to work it out. 'So you think he's selfish, or mean, or you don't share the same interests?'

'No,' she said, and she took a deep breath, as if she was about to tell me she'd gone off with his best friend, but what she actually said was, 'I don't like his clothes.'

I nearly laughed. I settled for a smile.

'And that's why you don't want to go out with him?'

'I know it's stupid, and I've tried to tell him, but I can't, because it sounds so mean and superficial, so I suggested we went shopping, and I pretended it was for me, but when we got there I was going to point out good stuff for him, and maybe that would have given him the idea, or maybe I could have suggested getting him something, but he wouldn't go and I just suddenly felt I couldn't be with him for another minute while he was wearing those trousers.'

They're combats. Max has been wearing them every day since he got them for his birthday. I mean every day. Mum has to steal them in the night to wash them. I realised this was relevant. Not the washing, the wearing.

'But he must have worn them on your first date?'

'Yeah. I didn't like them then, but I thought I could change him. I was wrong.'

I was worried that she was going to cry, which would be dead embarrassing, so I had to do something.

'Can I use your phone?' I asked.

She nodded, holding the tears in.

'It's your trousers,' I said to Max on the phone.

'I like them,' he said defensively, as if I were Mum asking to wash them.

'Liz doesn't.'

'Let me speak to her.'

I handed the phone over to Liz. There was a short silence and then she smiled and said, 'So when do you want to go shopping?'

I left quietly. I would let him thank me later. Ideally by buying me a new computer game, but I would settle for a couple of his old CDs.

I was just about to go when I remembered Sam lived in the same house. Of course I knew that really, because I'd been visiting it since I was a foetus, but it was so long since I'd been round to see him properly I'd almost forgotten that was what I used to do. We'd spend hours playing games, watching TV and eating. We hardly talked at all but we were so happy to be with each other. Since I'd started the club we'd hardly spoken, except to say difficult things. Would this have happened without the club? Was life tricky simply because we were twelve and two-thirds? I would never know.

I nearly fainted when I saw Sam. He was wearing a pair of combat trousers. Perhaps he had got the idea from Max. Perhaps this meant that he secretly had a girlfriend he wanted to annoy. Or perhaps he'd wear them for a few years, get a girlfriend who liked combats and then annoy her by going back to jeans.

He was stuffing the pockets with a torch, a waterproof, food, drink and, bizarrely, a comb. Everything you'd need for a week in the Orkneys.

'Where are you going?' I asked.

'Natalie's,' he said sternly, and then dropped to the floor and did some press-ups.

'Are you starting work on the new pigsty?'

'No, I'm going to sleep in the old one.'

He's gone, I thought. Trying to create artificial intelligence has caused him to lose his own.

'What are you doing that for? To experience the lifestyle of a pig, so you can build them a better sty?'

'I'm doing it for Natalie.'

He may be bonkers, I thought, but as least he's chatty with it. This was the most direct discussion we'd had in years. There was no stopping us now. I asked him straight: 'Have you fallen for her?'

'Big Bob has. He's asked her out.'

He picked up some big black gloves and pulled them carefully on to his hands. I felt cold and ever so slightly sick.

'Is that what he was doing in the playground?'

'Yup. He's very direct.'

Sam pulled on his boots.

'So is Natalie.'

'Yup. She's told him she's not interested.'

'Good. I don't think he'd be much fun to go out with. He'd probably take you to the boxing.'

Sam pulled on a woolly hat.

'So why are you going to Natalie's?'

Sam looked straight at me. Little wisps of his ragged fringe were pushed down by his hat and fell into his eyes.

'I'm going to stop him.'

He marched out of the door and I followed him, like a puppy on the lead of an angry owner.

'Stop him doing what?' I asked, trying to keep up with his gigantic strides.

Now I felt like a toddler trying to keep up with a mother in a hurry (aren't they always?). It was so tiring, not just changing how I felt, but who I felt like. Or is it whom? I was too tired to think about grammar on top of everything else.

'Stop him doing *what*?' I repeated.

'He's made noises about the pigs.'

'Don't you mean *like* the pigs?'

'No, I don't.'

When we got to the farm the heavy metal gate was

shut. Natalie was on one side; Bob on the other. We couldn't hear what they were saying, but he seemed very insistent that he come in and she seemed very insistent that he stay out. At one point he grabbed her shirtsleeve and she pulled back and hit her fingers on the gate. She winced and sucked them.

We moved forward and hid behind a tree. I amazed myself by actually wanting to go and sort Bob out. I don't mean tidy his clothes, I mean rearrange his limbs. Not only did I *feel* like doing this foolish thing, I was actually prepared to have a go.

I was still scared of him, but I was more angry than scared. This surprised me. I thought fear would be more or less my only emotion for about the next five years, but it didn't feel right that someone strong and proud like Natalie should be fenced in by a blob like Bob. Predators belong in wildlife documentaries, not on Natalie's farm.

'Just try the boxing once. There's a bantamweight bout on Saturday. There won't be much blood.'

So he *did* like boxing.

Natalie looked as steely as the gate.

'I've told you, I *don't* want to go out with you.'

'How do you know? You haven't tried it.'

'I *know*. Just like I know I don't like fennel without trying it.'

'What's fennel?'

'Go away, Bob.'

He regarded her stonily. 'What a pity.'

'Not for me.'

She turned and marched back towards her planet-saving house.

'I fancy pork for tea tonight,' said Bob, darkly.

She stopped, of course, in her tracks, turned and looked anxiously at the pigsty.

'Or maybe a little bit of lamb.'

Now Sam was straining to unleash himself on Bob, but I held him back. Big Bob loped away from the gate, looking dark and gruesome even in the summer light.

We ran up to the gate. Natalie was walking away, all hunched and diminished.

'Natalie!' Sam called, in a shouting whisper.

Natalie spun round, looking so angry I thought she'd shoot poisonous beams of radiated light out of her black pupils, dissolving us into pools of melted boy. In fact she smiled as soon as she saw it was us.

'It's us!' croaked Sam unnecessarily.

She ran to the gate and opened it.

'Ring our parents and tell them we won't be back for a bit,' Sam instructed her, as he stomped over to the pigsty.

The pigs considerately moved aside. Sam spread out his

waterproof and sat down on half of it. I was clearly supposed to sit on the other half, so I did.

'Thanks,' said Natalie, and ran back to the house.

So few words, so much stuff. This was not Sam who fiddled in his pockets. This was not Sam who only looked you in the eye if he was trying to work out the optic nerve. This Sam had turned a very big corner. So big he would never find his way back to where he had been.

We waited in the dark. We ate all the food. I felt a bit queasy, partly from fear, partly because all the food was cake. Natalie waited in her room, unseen but watching.

He came about an hour later. He walked straight over to the pigsty, not because he could see us but because he knew the pigs were Natalie's favourites. Sometimes she even threatens to bring them into school. We leaned back against the wall of the sty. He pushed his head through the door, like a cat through a mousehole. The pigs squealed. They'd been fine with us, but they knew this guy liked pork. It was time.

I grabbed Bob's hair and pulled him down on to the straw. Sam sat on his shoulders to stop him getting back out of the sty, but we couldn't do much more because he was blocking the door.

Then we heard a rattle and whispers. I peered out of the

sty. It was Natalie and two of her brothers with the wheelbarrow. The little one tried to handcuff Bob's ankles with useless broken toy handcuffs, but a slap from Natalie soon got him pulling on Bob's legs, along with his brother and sister. They managed to get Bob out of the pigsty and we crawled along behind. I tried to grab Bob's arms, but he somehow wriggled free. He made for the gate.

Sam and I had only done one rugby workshop, but we knew enough to fling ourselves at his legs. We floored him, just as Natalie flew towards us with the wheelbarrow. The five of us somehow got Bob in.

With all our limited strength, and despite Bob's very imaginative swearing, we careered through the farmyard, got him over to the duck pond and tipped him in.

He screamed. Not yelled, or bellowed, or roared, which is what you'd expect of Bob. He screamed, like he was really terrified. It was only a duck pond – he wasn't going to drown or come across a shark. Then he did something which for anyone else would have been odd, but when big tough Bob did it it was almost funny. He flicked at his sopping arms and face and cried out, 'Get it off me! Get it off me. It's wet!'

I suddenly remembered something else wet. That little puddle in the playground at school. The one I'd splashed through just before Bob ran away from me. Of course. He wasn't running away from *me*. He was running away from the WATER in the puddle! Just like he was running away now from the water in the duck pond, squelching and sploshing down the street like a real wuss. We had to laugh. Well, we didn't have to, I guess. We just really wanted to, and we enjoyed it.

When I stopped laughing I noticed that Natalie had flung herself at Sam. I saw Sam's stocky hands creep out of his pockets and place themselves confidently around her waist.

For a moment I stood there, as if it were my turn next and it would be rude to go. But really I knew it would be rude to stay.

As soon as I got home, I had a bath, to wash off the pig pong. During the steamy soak I realised that it was the first time I'd ever had a bath without being asked to. Perhaps I had turned a corner too.

Chapter Eleven

The Circus

'Joe! Joe! You have to come! You have to see this!'

That was it, then. Sam had a girlfriend. He'd start washing for no reason, and going shopping, and giving little presents with bows (to her, not to me) and, worst of all, he wouldn't be available for my *Ivanhoe* video night.

I felt I'd lost him.

It was like when my granny died. Not Granny Jigsaw, who still comes to stay and brings the hardest jigsaws she can find. It was Granny Sweet who died. Sweet she was and sweets she brought. It was always liquorice allsorts, even though we don't like them. She always forgot. So every time she would then take us out to the sweetshop and buy something we did like. We used the allsorts for all sorts of games. At first it was playing shop, then they were cannons and bullets, then they were money tokens in card games (swapped for cash at the end of the game) and finally they were earrings, which she actually wore to pick me up after school.

When she died I got out some allsorts I'd kept. They were rock hard but not mouldy. I put them by my bed, with a photo of her, and got into bed with her letters. I had kept them in an old cardboard box that used to be a pirate treasure chest. They weren't really letters. They were notes and post-its. One she'd put in my lunch-box said, *Smile! Only three hours until we're playing football in the park*.

She wasn't always nice. She got really, really angry at least once every time she stayed. She screamed and shouted and forgot English words and started talking half in Greek, because she was born in Greece. Even the shouting wasn't too bad, because once she'd finished we used to do impressions of her and they made her laugh.

I didn't have any letters from Sam, because I'd seen him every day. I had some postcards from holiday: a photo of a sports car, one of a planet and one of a rare cow. Much better than the postcards adults send, which usually show a map of where they are. What's the point of that? They're already there and I'm not going.

I got out the postcards and a few photos: Sam and me dressed as Batman and Robin, Sam and me as Beckham and Owen, Sam and me as Sam and me.

I sat on my bed with the postcards and the photos. I narrowed my eyes, trying to make those times come back, but they wouldn't. I could hear Max's angsty music next door, so I pushed off the Sam stuff, lay back and listened. I felt like ringing Alex but it was too late.

I looked for Alex before school but he wasn't there. Sometimes, when the circus audiences have been low the night before, he has to leaflet the newspaper shops before he comes to school. I wasn't looking for Sam, because I assumed he'd be lolloping around Natalie in the girls' zone. I hung around for a bit, not looking at anything much. Big Bob crept gingerly into the playground. I noticed he had some marks on his neck, a lovely series of bruises – maybe the ducks had pecked him.

'Maybe next time he'll pick on someone who doesn't live on a farm.'

It was Sam. At my side. This proximity surprised me, as did the next thing he said. 'Can I come over tonight?'

It wasn't all over! Did this mean they weren't going out? Or had they gone out and split up in less than twenty-four hours? I believe these things happen. Before I had the chance to get the details, Natalie came marching up.

'I hope you don't think you're going out with me,' she barked at Sam.

'I don't,' he said defensively.

'Take that kiss back.'

'OK,' he said, and then, 'How do I do that?'

I felt a bit surplus to requirements. I wandered off, but not so far that I couldn't hear them.

'Just because you came and gave me a hand doesn't mean I'm a little damsel in distress!'

'I know,' said Sam. 'It would be hard for anyone to take on Big Bob without help.'

'I know,' she said, calming down a bit, 'but you've put me in a very difficult situation.'

We all are, I thought. People were staring at us as they went into school.

'I've taken back the kiss,' Sam said helpfully. 'We can pretend it never happened.'

For the first time ever, Natalie looked slightly unsure of herself.

'Yeah, but I want it back again.'

'The same one?'

'No, a different one. As equals. Not you being all heroic and me being all girly.'

The playground was nearly empty. I felt we should go in, but I also felt I shouldn't interrupt.

'OK,' he said. 'I'll never be heroic again.'

'And I'll never be girly,' she said happily.

It really was time for me to go now, and not just because school was starting. They kissed as the school bell rang. They were going to be very late for their first lesson.

Alex didn't come to school. I was worried. Maybe the show was doing really badly and he'd had to leaflet all day. Maybe they'd close early and move on. Or maybe he had a cold.

As soon as I got out of school, I went up to the heath to look for him. The circus had that quiet afternoon feel: most of the caravans were empty, but there were people hanging washing outside a couple of them, and the guard dogs slept under most of them, lazily lifting an eye as I went past. I could hear the band faintly from the big top. Alex had told me there were rehearsals every afternoon.

Alex's mum was doing a warm-up outside the tent, just like Alex was the first time I went up to the caravan. Alex looks very like her, though of course he doesn't have earrings and his hair in a ponytail. His mum smiled when she saw me and started talking in Polish. Then she popped into the caravan and emerged holding a bunch of leaflets.

'Alex,' she said, and pointed to the shopping centre down the hill.

'Right,' I said, 'I'll go and find him.'

It felt quite normal to talk to her in English, just like she talked to me in Polish, even though neither of us understood the other. I can even speak English to people who speak English and not understand a word they're saying.

Then she did a funny thing. She put her hand out and patted me on the shoulder and then winked as she said, 'Alex.'

I had no idea what she meant but it made me feel weird. I ran off to the shopping centre even though I wasn't really in a hurry.

I found Alex in a very long, thin newsagent's where there are so many sweets and newspapers that there isn't any room for customers. He was putting some leaflets down on the counter. As soon as he saw me, he walked out down the other aisle. I tried to get down my aisle but was blocked by a toddler choosing crisps. Eventually I climbed over him, got out of the shop and ran past Alex, who was going into the next one.

'Why are you avoiding me?' I asked, quite aggressively.

'Because I've let you down,' he mumbled back.

'You're letting me down by avoiding me,' I said.

'No, I'm not. I'd let you down even more if I were—' He broke off to ask the next shopkeeper if he could leave leaflets.

'If you were what?' I asked. This felt like the most important conversation I'd ever had, apart, of course, from the one I had with my parents when they split up, and split me up too.

'I've forgotten,' he said, and set off down the street again.

'I don't believe you,' I said, following him.

He looked down at the pavement, so fiercely I thought he could probably see through to the TV cables and the rats.

'I don't know why you're bothering with me. I told you I'd broken the rules of the club.'

'I'm bothering because—'

This wouldn't have been so hard to say if I hadn't been pacing and peering at the ground at the same time. We must have looked weird – as if we were looking for tiger tracks on a high street.

'Because you matter. To me.' There. I'd said it.

'Do I matter more than the club?'

'Of course you do!' I exclaimed. 'Anyway, the club's over. Natalie and Sam are an item.'

He stopped walking and looked at me.

'A kissing item?' he asked, with concern.

'I have witnessed it with my own eyes.'

'Oh. That's bad news.'

'Not really,' I said. 'It's actually quite a relief. So why don't you go out with the girl you like?'

'I can't,' he said, and started walking again.

'Why not?'

'I've told you before. I can't tell you.'

'But I'm your friend. Friends tell each other things.'

'I'm not a normal friend. I'll be moving on before long. You might never see me again.'

'That doesn't matter. You're here now. We're friends now.'

He was walking faster and faster. I couldn't keep up.

'Slow down, Alex.'

He suddenly stopped and turned to me. He put his hands on my shoulders.

'Pretend we never met, Joe. Pretend I was someone you saw in a bad film about a circus.'

Then he gave me a kiss on the cheek and sprinted up the hill.

Well. As so often in my life, I didn't know what to do. I stood there outside the shop, weighing up the fifteen or so choices I had, most of which involved some sort of running away. Then a strange thing happened – Dad came by. It wasn't strange that we met by chance – after all, we were near our house. But it was *extremely* strange because we were near the SHOPS. Dad only goes shopping every three years, and that's to get new boots. And today was the day. He was holding them in his hand. He doesn't believe in plastic bags.

'Stuck?' he said.

He'd just gone straight to the point and I was so amazed he'd *got* what the point was, I went straight to the point back.

'Alex just kissed me.'

'Where?' he asked.

'In the street.'

'I meant which bit of you.'

'Oh. Cheek.'

'Oh. Is that a problem?'

'Yes. He's a boy.'

'So? Maybe you're gay.'

I couldn't believe he'd said that outside the newsagent's. I couldn't believe he'd said it at all.

Unbelievably, he went *on*: 'Or, maybe Alex is?'

'I don't know.'

'Well, maybe you should find out.'

'He's leaving soon—'

'All the more reason to find out. Otherwise it'll be like reading a book and giving up before the ending.'

Alex wasn't in his caravan. His mother was sitting with her feet up, watching TV. I was surprised, because she had a show in a few minutes. Perhaps she warmed up by chilling out. When she saw me, she started jabbering in Polish, with actions and exclamations which reminded me of international wrestling. I hadn't got a clue what she was trying to tell me.

'Alex?' I asked meekly, hoping he could interpret.

She pointed wildly to the big top.

I walked over and peeped through the tent door. Everyone was getting ready for the show: the orchestra was tuning up, the hot dogs were sizzling, the programme seller was counting her change and fixing her wig. And in the centre, Alex was warming up. He saw me within seconds and pounded over.

'Go away! You're not allowed to watch!' he said, his dark eyes steely.

'Alex,' I said, quite angrily for me, 'I've had enough of you ordering me around.'

'Good,' he said, 'then you can go.'

'Alex,' the ringmaster called over, 'ten minutes!'

'You're going on?' I asked, surprised.

'Yes' he said nervously. 'My mum has had a big, big row with my dad and now she won't let him catch her.'

'Alex!' his dad called insistently.

'Can we meet after?' I quickly asked.

'OK, then,' he agreed, 'but *don't* watch the show!'

He bounced on to his father's shoulders and I left the tent.

*

As we were going to meet after the show, I decided to hang around. Cars began to drive shakily across the uneven ground. They were parked in funny zigzag rows by a large-shoed clown who pretended they'd run over his feet. Children got out of their cars laughing, which doesn't happen when you arrive at the supermarket or school. Some people arrived by bus, others on foot. Everyone, even the really grey and tired-looking grown-ups, seemed excited.

I leant on a car and watched, wishing I could stream into the tent with them, angry that I didn't even know why I couldn't. Was it that I would make him nervous? Was it that he thought he wasn't any good? Was it that he had a silly costume? I turned these possibilities over in my mind, kicking my heels in the already churned-up heath.

From far away, I saw four figures and recognised them immediately. It was Sam and Ben, Natalie and Marilyn. This wasn't what I needed. At least they weren't holding hands.

As they got nearer, I called out to Ben, 'No baby today?'

'What baby?' he said, vaguely.

'Marilyn's baby sister,' I reminded him. 'The one you've practically adopted.'

'Oh, that baby,' he said, and looked away. Maybe he thought it would be pushing its own buggy across the heath.

Marilyn smiled. 'We're not so bothered about the baby

now. It's sort of done its job.'

'What job?' I asked, thinking that babies were too young for office work.

'You know,' said Marilyn, smiling cheekily.

Suddenly I knew. Of course I knew. Ben would never have gone near Marilyn if it hadn't been for the butterflies and the borders. I should have been angry with her, but I was actually quite impressed.

Sam and Natalie were debating who should pay.

'You definitely owe me, after the pigsty trick,' he was saying.

'It wasn't a trick! My parents *might* want you to design one.'

'Yeah, but we don't know that, do we? After all that work you got me to do . . .'

'Yeah, but it was worth it, because you got to know me.'

They went over to the box office, still arguing.

I had to admit to myself that the girls had been dead clever. They'd got us into their lives even when we'd vowed we wouldn't let it happen. And they didn't even know about the club.

'Are you coming to the show?' Ben asked, daring to look me in the eye again.

'No, don't fancy it,' I lied.

It was nearly time for the show to start. As my friends

squeezed in with the last few stragglers, the programme seller shut the canvas doors.

I wandered up and down through the cars. I worked out people's lives according to their mess: dummies, bottles, picture books, soldiers, dolls, Travel Scrabble, story tapes and CDs. I guessed the age and gender of all the kids in each car.

The band started to play. There were fanfares, and drum rolls, and applause. I felt left out, but it wasn't a new feeling.

I was reading a comic upside down through a windscreen when I heard the ringmaster call out, 'And now, ladies and gentlemen, boys and girls, the amazing, the daring, the Bouncing Bobinskis!'

Big applause. I clapped quietly on my own. I was mad with Alex for not letting me watch, but I supposed it was the last thing I'd do for him, so I might as well do it.

Suddenly the doors of the big top were ripped open. Sam and Ben came tearing out and called over to me.

'Joe! Joe! You have to come!'

'You have to see this!'

Without thinking, I raced into the tent.

Chapter Twelve

Somersaults

It was me doing somersaults. Not my body, but my heart. I was head over heels and heels over head, and I felt like I'd never stand up again.

The Bobinskis were still on. My eyes readjusted to the bright lights and the dazzle of their sparkly costumes. They were making a tower with all five of them. Alex's dad at the bottom, hugely strong and impressive, clasped his son's ankles on his shoulders. The next two boys climbed up carefully, one by one, balancing against all the odds.

Alex was the last up. He did a few flips and somersaults while he waited his turn. Then he rubbed some powder into his hands, so he wouldn't slip when he leapt.

But it was me who leapt. It was me doing somersaults. Not my body, but my heart. I was head over heels and heels over head, and I felt like I'd never stand up again. Even if I did, I wouldn't be the same as I was a few minutes ago, before the somersaults.

As the white dust fell, I took a moment to make quite

sure of what I saw. The blue leotard and tights, the glistening sequins, the muscular, gymnastic body. All this was Alex, I knew this was Alex, but there was something else. This was not the Alex I knew at all. I took a deep breath before I even let myself think it.

Alex is a girl.

Alex is a girl.

Alex is definitely, definitely a girl.

She got to the top. There was huge applause, but not from me. My hands wouldn't move. They had gone on strike to compensate for my brain, which was doing overtime, trying to work it all out.

She bounced back down to the floor. I decided to go. She took a bow. I got to the door. She came forward to take another bow, to the edge of the circus ring. I don't know why, but I turned before I went out. And she saw me.

Earlier that day Alex had run away up that hill and now it was my turn to run away down it. I didn't run because I thought Alex was following me, I ran because I didn't know what else to do with myself. I didn't even know where to go, so I didn't decide. But I found myself running back home, up the stairs and into Mum's kitchen. Mum was chopping vegetables. I sat down on one of the stools, panting. I broke the news to her, panting.

'Alex is a girl.'

'I know,' she said, without looking up.

'How do you know?' I said, outraged.

'Because of her mannerisms, and her body language, and the way she looked at you . . .'

The last bit was too scary to take on. I got cross instead.

'Why didn't you tell me?'

'I didn't think it would help. I thought if she wanted to tell you, she would. And if you needed to find out, you would. Which you have.'

This all sounded far too neat.

'Yes, but,' I blustered, 'I've spent the last two and a half weeks sharing my ideas about girls *with* a girl!'

'Best person to share them with, I'd have thought.'

I can't stand it when my mum's like that – all wise and knowing. I know she's been my age, and loads of other ages as well, but at least she could pretend she doesn't know the answer to everything. Then she said something terrible.

'Are you going to go out with her, then?'

'No, I'm not!' I cried out, and ran from the room.

I hadn't done so much running for a long time. I ran down the stairs, and down the road, but I didn't run all the way to the castle. I got the bus.

I walked round the moat. Round and round. Probably

more times than I've ever walked round it before. I thought back over the short but busy time I'd known Alex and little truths fell into place, one by one.

I realised that she pulled at her jumper because of what was underneath. I realised that she wouldn't sleep over because it would be hard not to change her clothes in front of me.

The more I thought about Alex, the more clues there had been. Clues to her being a girl. She probably didn't want to do rough and tumble because I might land on the wrong bits of her and find out what shape they were. Maybe because Alex was a girl she was more into Marilyn's baby sister. Maybe if she'd invited me into the caravan, I might have found out – from photos or clothes, or her parents. She can't have pretended she was a boy to them, but did they know she'd pretended she was a boy to me? I raced through the memories of the last weeks, as if I were rewinding a video at double speed to find a good bit, and remembered the way Alex's mother winked at me. It wasn't because she had fallen for me. It was because Alex had.

Was I the person Alex said she liked but couldn't tell me about? I had to stop walking to think about this one. It was such a big question, I knew walking wouldn't bring the answer. I might as well have a break, at least from the walking. I'd had too much to think about to keep count, but I'd probably been round a hundred times. I'd had to change direction because I felt dizzy.

I gazed at the goldfish. I wanted to dive in and join them. Their lives couldn't be this complicated. For a start, a girl goldfish couldn't pretend to be a boy goldfish, because they all look the same. Or maybe that means they could?

I couldn't think about this little question any longer, because another question was coming along, like a huge surfing wave, much bigger than all the others that had landed on me: why had she done it?

A bell rang. It wasn't like the loud electric school bell. It was a bell rung by hand, by the hand of the castle curator. It means the castle shuts in ten minutes. I looked up to see if it was the grumpy one who complains about litter or the nice one who bought me the bow and arrow and who's seen every film version of *Robin Hood* and is happy to talk about them. It was the grumpy one. Of course.

Then I saw Alex. She was riding her horse again. She leapt off in her usual impressive way and walked towards me along the lawn at the edge of the moat. She was still dressed as a boy. Actually, she could have been dressed as a girl, because she was wearing jeans, a sweatshirt and trainers, which everyone wears, even my granny. She looked really good. In fact, she'd always looked really good, but now I knew she was a girl, it was a different sort of really good. She still had short black hair and very dark eyes and pale skin and a wide mouth, but I was looking at her in a new way.

I'd always thought she was handsome, as a boy, but the same face with different information made her look different – better. If you call beautiful better, which, in the case of Alex, I do. She got close enough to talk.

'How did you know I was here?' I asked.

'You always come here when you've got troubles.'

'You think you're trouble?'

'Yeah. I'm sorry.'

I asked my big question. 'Why did you do it?'

'Because I didn't want to be a girl.'

'Don't you like being a girl?'

'I did. Until I got old enough to go out with boys.'

'So you don't like boys?'

'Yes, I like boys, but not the idea of going out with them.'

'Sounds like how I am about girls.'

'Yeah.'

We both smiled, and then looked at our feet, because it was so much easier than looking at each other's faces. Muddier, but easier.

A light-bulb went on in my head, but it was one of those ecological ones that are really dim. I had to check with her I'd got it right.

'Did you pretend to *be* a boy so you wouldn't have to go out with one?'

'Yup. I was scared.'

'So was I,' I admitted.

'I've only done it once, at your school. My parents don't speak English, so I filled in the application form and when I got to 'sex' I just put 'boy'. I hadn't decided to do it beforehand, but once I'd done it I had to act it out.'

'Did you want to swap back?'

'Not at first, because I met you, and found out about the boys' club, and it all worked really well, but then . . .'

She started walking and I fell in step with her. There's only a limited time you can look at your shoes, so then we looked straight ahead instead. As she didn't finish her sentence, I finished it for her:

'. . . things changed.'

'Yup.'

'It was good we got the chance to know each other, without the boy-girl thing getting in the way.'

'Yup.'

We had arrived back where Monika the horse was standing patiently. I stroked her nose (Monika's). I don't know why – I never normally do that kind of thing, but it felt soft and warm and nice.

'Do you want a lift?' Alex asked.

'Yeah – please,' I replied.

She gave me a leg-up on to the horse and then leapt up herself. She gave me a spare riding hat out of the saddle-bag, then helped me do up the strap. I always thought it would feel really awkward, a girl doing a thing like that, but it felt fine. She put on her own hat and she looked great.

'Your eyes are so deep I want to jump in and swim in them,' I muttered.

'Who said that?' she asked.

'Max to Liz, and me to you.'

'Just because I'm a girl, doesn't mean we have to go out,' she said gently.

'I know,' I said, and I did know, at last.

'Do you want to go out?' she asked.

'Aren't you going away?' I asked back.

'Is that an answer?'

'It's a question.'

'Mum wants a break. She and I are going to stay for a while.'

We both smiled.

'Great,' I said.

'Still doesn't mean we have to go out.'

'Don't you want to?' I asked.

'I don't know. It might spoil things. Do you?'

'I don't know,' I said. 'Shall we wait and see?'

'Yeah. Wait and see.' She smiled. 'Ready?'

I smiled and nodded. She twitched the reins and Monika set off. I put my arms around Alex's waist, partly for safety, partly because I wanted to. And it felt fine. It all felt fine. I could touch her and laugh with her and smell her and talk to her and be with her. She was a girl and I was a boy and we were friends. Maybe one day we might be more than friends. I didn't know, but I wanted to find out. Not yet, though. For now, I wanted to enjoy the moment.

Monika clattered over the bridge. I tightened my arms around Alex's waist, but not because I was scared. Everything was fine. It was all absolutely fine.

I'm glad I met Alex.